Promises To Keep

Jada Pearl

Acknowledgements

This book is dedicated to my angels: My parents Billie and Ernest, Billie Mae Napier, and my twin sister, Meco Carleen Whitaker. Thank you for continuing to watch over me always. Love you and RIH!

This sticks with me constantly "Don't ask God for direction if you don't plan on moving your feet." So each day I give God much deserved praise for waking me up daily and giving me an opportunity to get it right and create.

To my sons, Quentein (Nylah) and Alvin Jr. for always being so supportive of my work. I love you both. To Gloria, Tricia, Darenda, Latonya, Ta-Nisha, To-Nesha, Ashley, Octavia, Tyra, Tina, Sonia, Monique, Kenya R., Joy M., and Shaneen: the strand you all uphold on my rope, whew I can't say thank you enough. Thank you to the rest of my huge family and friends for the encouragement and support. Special thanks to AWAOA, Tenita, Cynthia, Felecia: you rock!! Last, but not least, thank you always to my readers for sticking by me and being patient as I create.

Home Sweet Home

Tarilyn pulled up to her brother's house and turned
the ignition off. She looked around the familiar
neighborhood. It was filled with decorative lights and
scenic Christmas displays. She blew out a hard breath and
looked at her hands as they were on the steering wheel. It
had been six years since she had been back to Detroit. Even
this visit wasn't her choice, but her mother had been
diagnosed with cancer, and said she wanted all her kids
home for Christmas.

She had to be here. Glancing in the rearview mirror
she looked into the back seat at the gifts she had brought.
She was sure her nieces and nephews would be pleased.
Why was she so nervous? Her hands were literally shaking.
She rubbed them on her jeans and decided she needed to
get inside before she pulled off.

It was only her family, but weren't your family the
ones who were always the most critical? Tarilyn didn't
look the same as she did the last time, they all saw her. She
just wasn't sure how they were going to react. Over the last

three years she had worked on her weight and her looks. She used to weigh close to 265 pounds, and on her five-foot four height, it was a lot. It took her to have a health scare for her to get serious about losing the weight. She didn't even tell her family about the health issue that had almost disappeared. No one in the family had seen her since she'd lost over a hundred pounds. No pictures, nothing. She let her hair grow and it was now to her mid back. She wore it straight and had recently dyed it light brown. She was also wearing a little makeup.

Makeup was something she never wore, well nothing more than eyeliner and lip gloss. Now she added eyeshadow and sometimes, color on her cheeks. Her dimple in her left cheek always stood out to her. She grazed her face and then sucked her teeth hunching her shoulders slightly. Just as she was about to open her car door, she was suddenly blinded by headlights from a vehicle behind her. She waited a few seconds, until the car cut its engine and the street went dark again. She went to open her car door again.

Stepping out, she reached for the back-door handle so she could retrieve the packages from the back seat. She was distracted by the noise coming from the car that had pulled up behind her. The couple, who she still couldn't see clearly were having a heated discussion. Trying to mind her own business but wanting to let them know they were being heard, Tarilyn slammed her car door a little harder than needed, to let them know someone else was outside with them. The couple stopped arguing and looked in her direction. Tarilyn was surprised to see it was her sister, Tanisha. She didn't know who the man was because last she knew her sister wasn't dating anyone.

Waving, she nodded and then headed to the door. As long as he wasn't putting his hands on her sister, she didn't feel a need to intervene. Taking the steps two at a time, she reached the top when the door was flung open, "Auntie Tari. You made it!" her nephew Caleb screamed, reaching his young eight-year-old hands to help her with the packages. Even though Christmas was a week away, she didn't want to have the stuff at her hotel.

"Hey, Caleb. Thank you but be careful with those okay."

"Okay, I will. Hey everybody Auntie Tari, is here," her nephew announced as she grabbed a hanger and placed her coat into the closet.

She waited for a few seconds to see if her sister and friend were coming. Within one minute, her sister came sauntering in alone. She would have to ask what that was about later. "Hey, baby sis. It's so good to see you. Damn you look good girl, I am almost jealous," Tanisha told her, hugging her. Tanisha was about two inches over her. She was the one with the figure that men always loved, she was kind of top heavy, with a thick waist and big butt. She had long locs in her hair and they were a dark and light purple, her favorite color. They weren't the same complexion, she was a shade lighter and Tanisha had a different eye setting then hers. She has slanted eyes were Tanisha had exotic looking eyes like their mama.

"Love your hair color. I see you changed it up a little and you know it's good to see you too. Where's your friend?"

"Oh please, he ain't ready to meet this family. He was just dropping me off, since my car is in the shop."

"Oh, okay… but are you okay? You two were going at it kind of tough," she asked her sister, with a look of concern on her face.

"Oh yeah, I am good. You know how I do. He is mad, because I wouldn't let him come inside. He thinks I got someone else meeting me here. So, no worries. He will be alright, trust me."

"Okay. Come on. I want to sit down; I have been driving for a while." Tarilyn told her sister as they walked further into the house.

The room they were heading into suddenly erupted in loud cheers. Her brothers were both seated in front of the television watching the Detroit Lions play a rare Thursday night game. Tarilyn watched them for a moment. She missed them. She looked around the huge living room and it was filled with pictures of all her family. She was the youngest of four. Her two brothers both were married and had three kids each. Tanisha never had kids, she said her nieces and nephews were enough for her.

The only person missing was Tarilyn's son, Tion. He had finals and wouldn't be coming to Detroit until Christmas Eve. Michael and Maurice could have been twins, they were over six feet tall, and they were both a shade or two darker than Tarilyn and Tanisha. She could tell they had gained weight some, but it didn't look bad on them, just proved they had wives who just so happened to be sisters. Michael was the oldest. He had a beard and a goatee that was now showing some signs of gray, and he looked distinguished.

Maurice wore a bald head and just a thin mustache. He had a small limp due to a sporting accident when they were in high school. She loved her brothers and sister, but she always felt a little bit out of the loop with them though. She was always the thickest and her hair was a different texture than Tanisha's. Tarilyn could recall asking her mother about the differences, her mother always just brushed her off without fully answering her. She just let it go eventually. Clearing her throat she spoke,

"Hey Michael, hey Maurice, where's mom?"

Both brothers broke free from the television, looking at her with their mouths open. Slowly they came over to give her a hug. This is exactly what she had feared and why she was so nervous. She didn't walk in the door the sister they were all expecting, she knew her transformation would shock them, but she didn't want them to make a big deal, even though it was a big deal. When they finally finished staring at her, her oldest brother Michael spoke,

"Tari, you look so beautiful. Not that you weren't before, but I almost didn't recognize you," he told her. Tarilyn blushed.

"Thank you Michael. Trust me it was hard… but with Tion helping me, I had to start somewhere. It was done first by changing the way I ate, then I started walking, and using the treadmill," she told her brother.

Maurice was a year older than her, closing his mouth he finally spoke.

"Yeah, sis you look great. I am proud of you. I think mom is either in the kitchen with Nicole and Stacy, or she is lying down."

"Yeah, she still tries to cook or better yet, watch over the ladies to make sure they do it right as she says," Michael told her. "It is so good to have you home."

"Thanks, Michael. Right now, it feels good to be home."

Both brothers hugged her and went back to their game. She turned and left to look for their mother. In the distance, she could hear them complimenting her. Smiling, she went into the direction of the kitchen, and could hear her sister-in-laws talking. She stopped. She really wasn't planning on listening to their conversation until she heard her name. Nicole was talking,

"So no one has seen her since she slimmed down. I heard it's a drastic change."

"Yeah, but I don't know why she did it. I thought she was comfortable with her look, I mean it runs in their family. It wasn't like she was that overweight, was she? Their whole family has those big boned genes. Look at Michael, he works out all the time, and he is just buff." Nicole said.

"Right, right. I can't wait to see her, though. Do you think she knows about the other stuff yet?"

"I don't think so. Michael said he didn't want to be the one to tell her, as far as I know Tanisha, or Maurice, haven't said anything either."

"Well, I hope things don't get too intense because of it but she does deserve to know," Stacy said.

Feeling as if she heard enough, Tarilyn opened the door at that moment and both women looked at her wide-eyed.

"OMG! Tarilyn… you look… you look amazing. When did you get here?" Nicole asked her as she was recovering from the shock of seeing how different her sister in law looked.

Drying her hands off, Nicole hugged her, followed by Stacy. Both women still had their mouths agape. Tarilyn was kind of used to this lately but they were making her a little uncomfortable. "I just got here, I was looking for ma."

"Oh, she went to lay down about an hour ago. She is in the den. I have to agree with Nikki, you do look amazing."

"Thank you both. It was hard but I had help. Let me go check on mom, I will see you two later and we can catch up," she said, walking back out the door she came in. Nicole was a few years older than her but was also the older of the two sisters. They were biracial with green eyes and glowing skin. Nicole wore her hair always in a ponytail or clipped. She never wore it down outside of the day she married Michael. Stacy had cut hers off and wore hers short and curly. Stacy also had a face full of freckles, and so did all of their kids. It made her stand out. Tarilyn got out her thoughts as she heard them continuing to talk, she didn't even bother to stand there and listen. She knew they were talking about her again. Although she did wonder what they were talking about and what it was that she needed to be told. What were they keeping from her? Was her mother worse off than she was led to believe? She wondered. She

12

was almost at the den when Caleb and Michael Jr, ran up to her.

"Auntie Tari, you look different, but you look pretty. And oh yeah, we didn't get our hugs and kisses from you," the boys rattled off at her one after the other. She laughed and quickly forgot her original thoughts as she scooped up five-year-old, Michael, Jr., She then went down on one knee, as she hugged him tightly and slobbered him with kisses. He started laughing at her antics. Caleb jumped up and down excitedly, "Okay, it's my turn, it's my turn."

She put Michael, Jr. down and Caleb flew into her arms. She repeated her hugs and kisses she gave to the younger child, and Caleb laughed loudly. She missed this, Tion barely let her kiss him these days. He told her he was too old for all that, but she knew he loved the affection. She always made sure he was shown affection, because her parents didn't show much towards them. Even though they were a close knit family back in the day, they were never showered with hugs and kisses. She stood up and the den door was yanked open. "What is all this racket out here?" her mother asked, and the boys went running off down the hall. Tarilyn laughed, "Hey mom. Sorry. It's my fault I was just showering them with some hugs, and they got over excited."

"Hey baby girl, it's okay. I wasn't sleep anyways. I was wondering when you would get here. How was the drive?"

"It was decent, but long. Gave me a lot of time to think. So how are you doing? You look tired ma."

"Now don't start fussing. That's not why you are here. Stand back let me look at you. That weight loss sure agrees with you."

"Thank you ma'. I feel good for the first time in a long time. We never know how much extra weight can affect your health, but at least the weight loss meant I didn't have to have that original planned surgery."

"Good. Good. How much did you lose total?"

"116 pounds," she told her as her mother motioned for her to swirl around. She laughed. She did have to admit that the weight loss gave her some of her self-confidence back. Medically she was considered obese, but to everyone else she was just very thick. Now she was comfortable in a size ten. It's funny how her mother's approval was all she was looking for. Now that she was okay with what she saw, she was finally able to relax. Her mother took her by the hand and led her back into the den, closing the door behind them so they could have some privacy. She sat down on the couch, and then patted the seat cushion next to her. Tarilyn sat down. She looked at her mother, again thinking how tired she looked. Her face was filled with lines and her eyes were sad. Her usually glowing skin looked pasty, her mother had lost way more weight than Tarilyn. She was almost to the point of being frail but Tarilyn didn't dare say any of her thoughts to her mom. Instead, she braced herself for whatever her mother was about to talk to her about. She immediately thought back to what she had heard earlier. Was that what she was about to discuss?

It Only Takes A Minute

Tarilyn's mother squeezed her hand and then reached for the other. She immediately took a deep breath closing her eyes and then opening them right back up. Tarilyn watched her in confusion but hoped what she was thinking didn't show on her face. This couldn't be good at all.

"Tarilyn I wanted to be the one to tell you that the doctors said my cancer has spread more than they thought, they want me to start chemotherapy. Well actually they wanted me to start last week, but I told them I wouldn't start anything until you were here. So do you mind going with me tomorrow?" Her mother asked.

"Mom, of course I will go. Why wouldn't the others go with you?"

"Tarilyn... because they don't know. Only you do, and that's the way I want to keep it."

"What? What do you mean?" Tarilyn thought back to what she overheard in the kitchen. If they didn't know that means this wasn't what they were talking about.

"Tarilyn Elyse, I said they don't know, and you bet not tell them. They can't handle things like you can. They my children and I love them, but you have always been the stronger one out of the bunch."

"Am I? I will do as you say ma, but you have to promise me that you will tell them if this progresses worse than it already is."

"We will talk about that when the time comes. I also want us to go see my lawyer when we leave the doctor's. I already went and made you executer of my will and estate. Everything is finalized. I just want you to get a copy of everything, and make sure there is no bickering over stuff, and before you even start my decision is final. Michael's wife has him soft now, so I don't want to be bothered with all that. You always act like the oldest anyways, you got way more sense than they do. Don't be looking at me like that child. I said I have made my decision on this okay?" her mother told her.

Tarilyn just nodded, what was she supposed to say with her mother hitting her with all this at once? She opened her mouth to ask a question and then closed it, deciding to keep quiet. She didn't want her mother to see her cry, so she held her tears in as best as she could. They sat in silence for a few moments when she heard the kids yelling it was time for dinner. She squeezed her mother's hands and then she stood up, bringing her mother with her. Tarilyn wiped her mother's tears from her face, and kissed her mother, who suddenly looked even more tired to her. They walked hand in hand into the dining room. Everyone was looking at them when they got there. Smiling, she laughed lightly hoping to change her mood, "Okay, who's saying grace?" Tarilyn said in a made up cheery mood.

Michael stood up and everyone followed him as they stood up and joined hands. Within a few seconds, Tarilyn's nieces she had yet to see filed into the room taking someone's hands. They smiled wide-eyed at her but said nothing. Her brother bowed his head and they all did the same, and he said grace, "Father, bless the hands that have prepared this food for the nourishment of our body, and the nourishment of our souls, we ask that you provide strength to our family as we come together during this holiday season and give us the power to do and be better, in your name we pray."

"Amen" came from the table in unison. Everyone sat down and the table exploded in chatter. Her nieces came over and gave her high fives and kisses as mama was served first, and then the plates and bowls were passed around. Tarilyn had just put a piece of broccoli in her mouth when her niece Micah asked where her cousin was. "Tion has finals, but he will be here by Christmas Eve,"

Tarilyn told her. Tarilyn shook her head "no" on the bread, and the mashed potatoes that were passed around and offered to her. "Wow, so you don't eat real food anymore, huh?" Nicole asked her.

"It's not that. I just eat my food in better consumption. Changing the way I eat is better for me overall. So please don't be offended if I turn down certain things," she explained to her family. No one said anything so she just finished off her vegetables and water as she quickly felt full.

Darlene was deep in thought as she looked around at her family. Having Tarilyn home was all she really wanted and needed right now. She loved all her kids. They all had that something about them and had very different personalities. *"Raising them was definitely a job,"* she thought while she looked from each of her children. They all were the same complexion outside of Tarilyn. She was more of a light brown to their medium brown. In fact, she favored Darlene's sister who was in fact, her real mother. Tara was her youngest sister, but she died while she was giving birth to Tarilyn. She always wondered why the others never grew suspicious of it, but maybe it was because of her size. Only three people knew of this secret that she kept. She never got to say goodbye to her baby sister, and she was the only person left alive holding it in her soul, at least that she knew of. Her mother and her husband Marvin, God rest his soul were both deceased now. Tarilyn's father, Darnell knew but only God knew where he was, he never came around after Tarilyn turned five. He said she looked too much like her mother, claiming he couldn't handle it. It was too much for him. Tara was only seventeen when she gave birth, and he was twenty when she died. The doctors had said that the childbirth was too much on her young body. If it wasn't for mama helping her out with all of them, and the financial support Darlene received from Darnell, they wouldn't have been able to take care of four kids on their own. All her kids themselves were stair steppers, but Marvin was a great father to them all. She missed him so much. That drunk driver would never know how much he took from their family. Quickly wiping a tear from her face before any of them saw her, Darlene suddenly became tired and now she needed to lay down from all this thinking. Pushing back from the table she stood up and the conversation at the table immediately came to a standstill. Darlene noticed that everyone was watching her. Tarilyn was the first to engage and immediately stood up as she went over to her, "Ma, are you okay?" she asked with obvious concern in her face. "Yes, chile' I am fine, I am full, and I am tired. I am going back to bed, I will see you in the morning, my appointment is at ten. Good night everybody, and boys, no noise!" she said to everyone at the table, as she gave her grandsons a look which meant she was serious.

Sitting back down, Tarilyn watched her mother take the stairs slowly until she was out of her view. She sighed heavily as she turned back around to her family. The energy in the room had shifted. Mostly everyone was finished eating now, so the girls had started clearing the table. Picking up her own plate and cup, Tarilyn started to help. Nicole stopped her, reaching for a glass she'd poured wine into. "Here take this glass of wine and go sit down somewhere. This is the girls' normal duty. They got this and don't need your help," she told her, smiling.

"Are you sure?"

"Yes, we are," Stacy chimed in, "Now go on and talk to your brothers and sister." Tarilyn thanked them and smiled at her nieces who were moving about the dining room. As the wives went into the kitchen, directing the kids, she then went into the other room with her siblings as she was directed. She felt like they were waiting on her.

She needed to find out what they knew or didn't know, and maybe find out more about what she overhead earlier. Standing near Michael, she sat the glass down on the end table without touching its content. Looking from one of her siblings to the next she took note of their facial expressions, which all seemed like they didn't know who was going to talk first. Getting impatient, Tarilyn addressed them. "Okay, out with it. What's really going on? What am I missing here? I feel like mom isn't telling me everything, so please somebody tell me something," Tarilyn finally sat and waited for one of her siblings to say something. They all looked from one to the other and then her brothers put their heads down. What the hell was going on, that no one wanted to tell her anything? Tarilyn absent mindedly grabbed her wine glass as she stood up again, walked, and stood in front of Michael. "Mikey. What are you all keeping from me?" she said, softly calling her brother by the nickname only she called him. Michael looked up at his baby sister and the tears started falling from his eyes. She had only seen him cry one other time, and that was at their father's funeral. This couldn't be good. She looked to her other siblings and Tanisha and Maurice, both were crying as well. Tanisha stood in the middle of the room completely upset. Finally, she took her sister by the hand and started to talk.

"Tari. Ma is. Ma is…" she started but couldn't finish because she was crying too hard.

Maurice wiped his face, and cleared his throat, letting out a long hard breath he spoke.

"Ma's cancer is worse than she has told you or us. She has stage four pancreatic cancer, and it has spread to her other organs, the doctors are saying she may not even make it to the end of the year. She… she doesn't know that we know, but Nicole found the doctor's note she had laying around and showed it to Michael. We are sure that was a complete mistake, but she forgets things now more than she ever did."

"What? What are you saying?" Tarilyn said as she suddenly felt dizzy.

Her brother grabbed her arm and led her back to her seat, taking her wine glass from her hands and placing it on the cocktail table. Tarilyn closed her eyes and willed the room to stop spinning. Tarilyn's thoughts went back to what her mother told her not even two hours ago. Why did she tell her all that if it wasn't true? She couldn't lose her mother.

She thought she was going to have a chance to fight this cancer. She wasn't ready for this. No, they didn't know what they were talking about! She was going to her mother's appointment tomorrow to speak to the oncologist and get some answers herself.

After about 20 minutes Tarilyn and her siblings had gotten themselves together enough to finish discussing her mother more. She was all out of sorts mentally and physically as they talked until almost midnight. Deciding it was time to go, she headed towards the staircase to look in on her mother before she went back to the hotel. Knocking lightly on the door, she opened it. She was surprised to see her mother sitting up reading a Bible. Darlene smiled weakly, putting the book face down on her lap as she watched Tarilyn enter the room.

"I thought you were asleep. I was just coming to check on you before I went back to the hotel."

"I tried to sleep but I was in some pain, so I decided to do some praying. Come sit down for a second."

Tarilyn did as her mother asked as she sat lightly on the bed. Her mother took a breath and winced in pain. How was it possible that her mother looked like she had aged ten years in the last hour? Tarilyn willed herself not to tear up.

"Do you need anything?"

"No. I just want you next to me for a second. You know I have tried your whole life to be a good parent to you, to your sister, and brothers. I know I didn't show you much affection, but you knew I loved you, didn't you?"

"Ma where is this coming from? Of course I knew. We knew. It's okay. You don't need to explain that to me now."

"Yes I do. You know we never talked about why you ran away from all of us...."

"Ma!" Tarilyn gave her mother a look, hoping it would stop the conversation. It was something she always hoped would not come up between them.

"Tarilyn, don't you use that tome with me! One day you will have to tell Tion about his father. I know all these years he has had some type of questions. Take it from me, secrets aren't good. They will find a way to come back and haunt you. Anthony is a good man. He just made a big mistake. His arrogance wasn't his entire fault. One day you will have to forgive him. He deserves to know he has a son. Tion is seventeen. He is almost a full man. That child deserves to know. They both do," her mother told her as the tears ran down her face.

Tarilyn was baffled on why her mother was so emotional talking about this. Why was she bringing this up now? They never talked about Tion's father. Mainly because she avoided talking about him after the way they ended. She never told Anthony about Tion and no one in the family said anything to him either. It helped that he didn't live in Detroit anymore. at least he didn't the last she knew. Anthony Robinson was her high school and college sweetheart, but he let basketball fame get to his head. He was always surrounded by females who didn't seem to care they were together, and he never made the effort to make them care. Tarilyn couldn't prove that he cheated and eventually she stopped wondering. When they graduated, they had a huge fight in front of their families because a girl walked up and kissed Anthony who did nothing but laugh it off. Tarilyn was furious and wiped her hands of him and their so-called relationship. She didn't look back nor forgive him and it wasn't because of the uncertainty and rude females. It was because he broke his promise. His promise to always make her feel loved and for her that was worth more than anything back then. She was always a loner and never felt pretty but he did manage to do that.

When he stopped making her feel that way, nothing else mattered to her. They were young. She got that, but it was just so much more to her. When she found out she was pregnant with Tion a month after graduation she wasn't happy or sad, but she knew she wouldn't tell Anthony. Her mother was upset with her, so when the job opportunity came with the advertising firm where she interned, Tarilyn jumped at it, not once looking back, and that's where she had been ever since.

The Reveal

Tarilyn currently was the Director of Marketing at her firm. She made a comfortable living, but she vowed that she didn't need Anthony, so she never sought him out. The last she knew he was playing ball with the New York Knicks. Did she think about it? Yes. The countless of unmailed letters she had in her home office drawer showed that. She just never could do it. Her pride and hurt always won. Tarilyn touched her mother's face as she came out of her thoughts wiping her mother's tears away. She lied back into the pillow. She started talking again, and Tarilyn had to lean over to hear her mother speaking because now she was whispering, "Don't make the same mistakes I made. I tried to do right by you, I tried to do right by you," she repeated.

"Mama, what's wrong? Please talk to me and tell me why are you all of a sudden saying all this? You are scaring me."

"Please just listen, if... if something happens to me, I have something for you in my safe. You still have the code, right?"

"Yes but Mama I don't want to talk about all this. You're going to be fine. We are going to your appointment in the morning, like you said, right?"

"Yes baby girl, we are. Yes, we are. I am tired now. I am going to rest. I will see you in the morning. I love you Tarilyn. I am so glad you came home to see me. One more thing, promise me, promise me you will tell him." Her mother said still whispering. Tarilyn wiped the last of the tears off her mother's face and pulled the covers up to her chin. Pausing, she just nodded. She didn't want to upset her with her being the way she was as she kissed her forehead and pulled her blanket up some more, just to have something to do with her hands. "No Tari, I want to hear you say it." Her mother said to her with pleading eyes, not knowing what else to do, she abided. "I promise mama, I will tell him." She said finally as she placed the Bible on the nightstand. Standing up, Tarilyn had a feeling in the pit of her stomach she couldn't explain as she looked back at her mother. Her eyes were closed, and she looked peaceful. Tarilyn watched as her chest rose and fell a few times before she finally hit the lights and closed the door lightly.

Tarilyn leaned against the door and slid down as the newly formed tears shook her body. Something wasn't right, but she couldn't do anything to change what was going on. This was one thing she couldn't fix. She brought her knees up to her chest and laid her head down, until she felt she had nothing left in her body to cry for. Was she crying for the things her mother said to her? Was she really being unfair to Anthony and to Tion? Her son was her everything. She didn't owe Anthony anything. At least that was what she told herself repeatedly when she thought about him. Tarilyn got up from the floor and began to walk away when she thought she heard voices coming from her mother's room. She started to open the door but was too afraid. She placed her hand on the door and the feeling in her stomach she had in her mother's room increased. Immediately, Tarilyn descended the stairs rapidly, barely feeling them under her feet. She needed to get out this house. She grabbed her coat, opening and turning the lock on the front door and ran to her car. She didn't even bother saying goodbye to anyone. She would text them so someone could finish the lock up. Getting into her car, she headed towards the hotel with so much on her heart and mind.

Tarilyn didn't even remember getting to the hotel or even into her room groggily she opened her eyes, looking to her side, what was that noise she was thinking as it woke her fully from her sleep. Getting her eyes to focus more she looked around the dark room finally realizing what the noise was. Her cell phone was ringing. Reaching over to the nightstand, she brought the phone to her face. It was still ringing pulling it back Tarilyn hit the green talk button, and spoke into the phone, "Hello?"

"Ma, Ma! Are you okay? Where are you? Why aren't you answering your text messages, or calls? Auntie Nisha has been trying to reach you."

"Uh, what? What's wrong?"

"She wouldn't tell me but told me to tell you to come back to the house now," Tion sounded really upset. Suddenly that feeling from earlier came back so hard, she dropped the phone and ran into the bathroom. She barely reached the toilet when the contents from dinner came up.

Once Tarilyn stopped throwing up, she rinsed her mouth out and grabbed her phone, "Tion, baby are you still there?"

"Yes mama, are you okay? What's going on?"

"Baby, I don't know, but when I find out I will definitely call you. Let me get over to the house okay." She told him as she dressed.

"Okay, mama, be careful and I love you," Tion told her softly into the phone. He felt he already knew just like she did. Her mother was gone. She felt it all through her body.

"I love you too," she told him. She ended the call and walked out the hotel front lobby. She finally looked at the time it was six fifteen in the morning. She had only gotten barely four hours of sleep, she cried the whole way to the hotel. Now she was starting to remember. When she got there, she went to the bar and downed three shots. Everything else after that was a blur until Tion called her.

Not Supposed To Happen

Gripping the steering wheel, Tarilyn drove to the house. She felt like her world was ending. Her mind was everywhere. Christmas was in six days, and this visit wasn't what she expected. Tarilyn jumped at the sound of the loud horn blaring behind her, she hadn't noticed the light turn green. She pulled off and within a few minutes she was on her brother's street. Immediately, she noticed the ambulance and Detroit police car out in front of his house. Her whole body shook as she had to park a couple of doors down. Neighbors were standing out in the cold curious as to what was going on. Getting out of her car, she walked slowly up to the house. When she reached the front porch stairs, she was greeted by her grieving sister, "She's gone, she's gone" she said to Tarilyn as she collapsed into her arms. Tarilyn held on to Tanisha as she cried hard onto her shoulder. Somehow, she was able to lead her back to the house and she sat her on the couch. Looking from one brother to the other, she noticed their silence. They said nothing with their wives on either side of them. Tarilyn wanted to see her mother. She needed to see for herself, she ran up the stairs and there were medical and police people around her. "Ma'am you can't go in there yet. Give them a few minutes please," the police officer, told

32

her softly holding her by the arm. Tarilyn didn't care what he said. As she broke free from his grasp and tried to run through, she was stopped by an EMS Tech, "Ma'am please", he said as he held on tighter. Tarilyn found strength she didn't know she had as she pulled away from him, rushed through the door, and landed at her mother's side of the bed. Falling on her knees, she grabbed her mother's slightly cold hand and placed it to her heart. "Mama, wake up, please, please you promised me. You promised me you would fight! You promised me, we were going to the doctor, please Mama wake up, I need you!" Tarilyn cried as the techs watched her in sorrow. She was glad they didn't do anything else to remove her, she needed to be next to her mother.

After a few minutes of her crying, she felt arms around her lifting her up. It was her brother. He carried her downstairs and into the room with the others. Tarilyn and her siblings all held each other and continued to mourn.

It had been two hours since their mother had been removed from the house. They called the funeral home they used for their father to come and get her body. The house was awkward and way too quiet. The children were all upstairs and Tarilyn was sitting on the bed where her mother once laid. Looking around the room, Tarilyn began thinking back to the conversation she had with her mother a few hours before. She looked over to where her mother kept the safe, she ran her fingers over the keypad while she closed her eyes and thought of the combination. Slowly she entered it in and the door clicked. Inside were a lot of documents, some things from when they were kids, and a lot of pictures of the grandkids. Moving some of the things to the side as she perused the safe, she finally saw the envelope with her name on it, it was pretty thick. She took it out and turned it over in her hand. She was just about to open it when she heard her name being called. It was her nephew, Michael Jr. Closing the safe she placed the envelope in her purse, getting up and then wiping her face off she turned around just as he opened the door, "Auntie Tari, are you in here?" his soft voice said.

"Yes, baby I am. Give me a second and I will be out okay?"

"Okay," he replied closing the door back lightly. He sat at the door waiting on his favorite aunt. He was scared to go into his grandma's room now.

Tarilyn straightened up her mother's bed and looked around the room. She knew unless she had to, this would be the last time she came in here for a while. She opened the door and looked down, and she was glad that she did. She saw Michael Jr. on the floor in the doorway, looking up at her with his sad eyes. Leaning down, she scooped him up. He held onto her neck tightly. They walked the hallway slowly as she rubbed his back, and then took the stairs, whispering to him. It was then she realized she hadn't checked her phone or called Tion back yet. When Tarilyn was midway down, she noticed his mother watching them. She handed him to her when they finally reached the bottom of the stairs, Michael took a hold of his mother's neck and she spoke, "There you are Michael. I have been looking for you."

"Mommie, I wanted to talk to Auntie Tari, I was waiting for her." He lifted his head and told his mother. Tarilyn nodded and kissed his forehead.

"I promise we will talk again today, okay?" she told him. He nodded right before he stuck his thumb in his mouth. Turning and exiting the room, Tarilyn walked to where she could have some privacy and dialed her son's number. He answered on the second ring. "Ma. What's going on, I have been waiting on you to call me back. Is everything okay?" Tion rattled off, before she could even say hello.

"Tion, honey slow down. Where are you?"

"I just walked in from school. Aunt Lisa picked me up after your text," he told her. Lisa was her best friend, and Tion was staying with her and her son.

"Okay, well Tion, your grandmother… your grandmother died in her sleep this morning," Tarilyn said through ragged breathes. She was okay until she had to say it again. She closed her eyes and willed the tears not to fall. She didn't want to upset him more than he already was.

"But I don't understand. I… I thought you said she was going to be okay," Tion said softly into the phone.

"Tion honey, I thought she was, but I guess she and God decided otherwise. I know this is hard for you. So, I need to know if you can finish up for finals later today or do you need me to call the school and have them extended for you?" she asked. She waited on the line until he was able to talk. Nicole walked past and handed her a cup of coffee. Tarilyn took it and mouthed, "Thanks." She'd texted Lisa right after they left with her mother and updated her on everything, having her call the school for her and inform them what was going on.

"Tion, baby are you there?"

"Yes…Yes I am here. Um, I will take the tests. I have one today and one on Monday, but I think if you or Aunt Lisa can call up there, I can take them both today. Then I want to fly to Detroit to be with you, is that okay?"

"Yes, that will be okay. I will call the school once I finish talking to your Aunt Lisa. Can you put her on?"

"Yes, and Ma, I love you, I will see you in a couple days, if you need me call me okay?" her son told her, as she felt his pain through the phone. Even with the distance, he always had spoken to his grandparents while he was growing up. Now he didn't have either of them. Tarilyn wished she could hug her son. She could hear him speaking to Lisa in the background. A few seconds later Lisa spoke, "Hey Tari. I am so sorry to hear about your mother. What do you need me to do?" Tarilyn spent the next 15 minutes talking to Lisa about changing Tion's flight and speaking with the school. When everything was taken care of she went to tell her sister she wanted to go back to her hotel room. Walking into the den, she saw Tanisha sleeping. Her brothers and their wives were sitting together talking. "Hey, I think I am going to head back to the hotel and makes some calls and try and get some rest, I will be back later this evening," speaking to them all at once. Michael looked at her with a strange look she didn't understand, but he nodded his head. Maurice had a paper in his hands that he handed to her without saying a word. Tarilyn took the paper from his hands and began reading. It was a letter to the family letting them know their mother had chosen Tarilyn as power of attorney and estate. It further explained that she would be in charge of all her mother's assets and arrangements. The letter was dated three months ago. "Where did this come from?" Tarilyn asked.

"Mama left it in her Bible, it was addressed to us all. We aren't mad she put you over everything, but we have been the ones taking care of her, since she couldn't stay alone," Michael told her. Tarilyn looked at her brother and thought she saw anger. *"Was he upset? even though he had just said he wasn't that he couldn't take of her arrangements?"* she wondered. "Michael, Maurice I would never not include you or Tanisha in whatever decisions need to be made for Mama. I didn't ask for this," she stated. Her brothers both nodded as if it made them feel better. Sighing heavily, Tarilyn laid the paper on the coffee table and headed to the door. She walked outside to her car, and the brisk cold wind almost turned her tears to ice. On the drive back to the hotel, she kept the radio off and thought about the conversation with her brothers. Why didn't her mother talk this over with them? Probably the same reason she didn't tell them everything that was going on with her. Reaching the hotel and parking, she headed straight to the elevators. After getting to her room and dumping her things on the chair, she sighed as she took the envelope out of her purse and headed to the chaise by the balcony door. Even though it was still light out, she just wanted the view.

Opening the envelope, she dumped the contents on the bed. Unfolding the letter inside, she started to read:

Tari, I always swore that this would go with me to my grave, and in a sense, it is but if you are reading this that means that I got my personal Christmas wish... to see you, and talk to you before I went home to be with my husband, mother, and sister. As you go through the papers in this envelope, know that I never meant to keep things from you, and that all I ever wanted was the best for you. I love you with my whole heart, and I hope someday you can forgive me, but please don't make the same mistakes I made. Let Tion meet his father and have a relationship with him. They deserve that, just like you do, no matter what the age.

Love your mama, Darlene.

Tarilyn reread the letter again with shaking hands. What was she talking about, why would she need to forgive her? Placing the letter down she unfolded the next paper, it was her original birth certificate. It wasn't the one she had at home. She read the parents' name and her hand immediately went to her mouth. Tarilyn's hand began to shake more as her eyes widened. She replayed in her mind what the birth certificate said. What the hell? Did she just read what she thought she did? Her parents weren't her parents. Tarilyn lifted the paper back up and read the names aloud, in clear black and white it said her parents were: *Tara White and Darnell Wilkinson*. Auntie Tara was her mother? Tarilyn tried to swallow but she felt like she had a ball of cotton in her throat. It explained a lot of things in her past and the things her mother said.

Family Lies, Family Ties

Why? Why didn't her parents tell her? Tarilyn wanted to be mad, but for some reason she knew this was what her mother needed to be at peace. How could she be mad, and she was doing the same thing? Tarilyn thought about her own question and then nixed even worrying about it right now. All she could think of was the hurt she was feeling for being left out the loop. Standing up and opening the sliding door, the cool wind hit her fiery skin. Her whole body felt hot with emotions, and her thoughts were racing. Then it came to her…Damn, how would she explain this to her siblings? Would she explain this to her siblings? She needed to think about that for a minute. It seemed her family had a lot of secrets in a matter of not even two days. She looked at the other things still sitting on the bed. Walking back over to them, she picked up another envelope and opened it. Inside were her mother's instructions and wishes for her funeral. She wasn't surprised to see that her mother had done mostly everything. What she was surprised to see was the law firm that was over her estate. The card read "Anthony Roberts, partner." The law firm was Williams, Roberts, and Donaldson. She wasn't surprised to see that Anthony was a lawyer, he was smart enough to be one. She just thought he would have continued his career in sports. She wasn't ready to see him, but now she had no choice. *"Her mother did this on purpose,"* she thought. This was her way of making sure she kept her promise at some point in her life. Grabbing her cell phone, she slowly dialed the number on the card and waited. When she heard him answer, she quickly ended the call. He sounded the same, but older, more masculine. The ringing of her phone scared her, and she jumped. *"Damn it,"* she thought, *"I must have called his cell phone instead of his office phone."* She hit the answer key on the third ring, taking a deep breath before speaking, saying "hello". "I'm sorry, I just got a call from this number and we got disconnected," he said into the phone. Tarilyn felt her mouth go dry. A flood of emotions came over her, hearing him talk. "Um, um…," she tried to say something, but her mouth wouldn't cooperate. "Hello, are you there?" he said, beginning to sound a little irritated. Getting herself together she tried to speak again, "Hi Anthony, it's me Tari," she breathed out in a bare whisper.

"Tari? Tarilyn, are you serious?" he said into the phone.

"Yes, it's me. I am sorry for that call. I... I..." she started but he quickly cut her off, "Tarilyn if you are calling

42

me, does this mean what I think it does? Where is your mother? Is she…" he stopped mid-sentence and seemed to wait for her to finish his sentence for him. "Yes, Anthony she passed this morning. I just got into town yesterday evening. We talked, had dinner as a family, talked again before I left for the night, but I guess that was all she needed."

"I am so, so sorry. Darlene and I… I mean Mrs. Johnston and I had become quite close over the last few months. I don't know what to say right now. Where are you? Are you at the house?

"No, I came back to my hotel room, so I could take care of some things. I guess I do need to take some time to see you since you are over her affairs," she told him.

"Yea, I guess so, which hotel are you staying at?" he asked. Tarilyn told him and they agreed to meet for a drink in the lobby in an hour. She ended the call and laid back on the bed. Too much was happening at once, losing her mother, and now talking to Anthony after almost 17 years. She wasn't ready for all this. Why did her mother think she was the strongest? Battling with her emotions, she wanted her mind to shut down because in all honesty she actually wasn't. She always had to hold her brothers

43

and sister down. They all came to her for money, advice, everything but who did she have to go to for the comfort? No one. Guess that's why she was strong. She didn't want to be the strong one anymore. She wanted to have someone to lean on for once. Her thoughts continued to rattle on. Looking at the ceiling, she knew that wouldn't happen. She let the tear drop go down the side of her face as it clogged her ear. At that moment, she had never ever felt so alone, not even when she had Tion, did she feel this way. Tion. What was she going to do about him and Anthony? That was something she still didn't want to think about at all.

She headed into the bathroom and turned on the shower. Tarilyn's body felt defeated and drained. Stepping in, she let the shower wash away the rest of her tears. This trip was not going anything like she thought it would. She got out, dried off, and started pulling her clothes out the drawer. She was running out of time. She couldn't decide how to dress, and finally opted for a pair of jeans and a sweater. It wasn't like it was a date. Walking into the bar, she spotted Anthony immediately. She stopped in her tracks when he stood and smiled at her. She was looking into the face of Tion but older. Walking towards one another, she smiled in return. "Wow you look amazing," Anthony told her as he leaned in and kissed her on her cheek. Blushing, Tarilyn didn't speak but took the moment to look at Anthony up close. He looked the same as when she last saw him, but he was starting to gray a little. It just made him even more handsome. Anthony was a caramel complexion. Standing tall at six feet three, he wore an earring in his ear. His square long face still gave him that modest look. He wasn't slim but he wasn't thick either, he held his own. He'd cut his facial hair off, she noticed. He used to wear a mustache and beard. Tion's was just shadowing in. *"Anthony must work out,"* Tarilyn thought. His eyes were his best feature, they were hazel with a tint of gold specks. They caught her attention back in the day. Even now, she found herself staring into them before she finally replied, "Thank you, you don't look so bad yourself."

"Thanks, do you want a drink, glass of wine?" He asked, all the while keeping his eyes on her. Why did it seem as if he had no problem with them sitting there, like it was something they did all the time? Tarilyn was a ball of emotions of the inside. She hated that she always went through all her emotions at once.

"I will have a glass of white wine please," she told him as she shifted in her seat. Anthony signaled for the waiter, placing their drink orders. "I am still in shock over

Ms. Darlene. I thought she would have pulled through all this."

"So, did I. How long were you her lawyer?" Tarilyn asked, wanting to change the subject. She sipped her wine, as he spent the next 10 minutes telling her how he had bumped into her mother at a friend's social gathering. What he said next almost made her spit out her wine. "Darlene told me about you living in Atlanta, and that you have a teenage son. I am happy to see you followed your dream and stayed with Zanders," Anthony said, after taking a long swig of his drink. Tarilyn watched his face to see if there was any type of emotion at the mention of "their" son. There wasn't. So that only meant that her mother didn't tell him how old he was. "Did she? ... and yes, I did. Funny she never mentioned she had run into you." He laughed. She smiled slightly but said nothing. He stopped and his expression became serious, "That doesn't bother you does it? I mean what happened between you and I was such a long time ago. I don't hold any hard feelings. I was the one that was wrong," he said, hoping to explain away her expression.

"Anthony, what we had ended over 15 years ago. It's in the past. I am not expecting anything from you," She told him. Anthony just looked at her. He grabbed her hand and massaged the back of it. "What if I wanted to rekindle what we had? Even before your call today, I have been thinking about you. I can't tell you how many times I looked at the number Darlene gave me. I just didn't want you to not want to talk to me," Anthony told her as he held her hand tighter. "What, Anthony? What are you talking about?" Tarilyn snatched her hand back. Giving him a look of pure bewilderment, she continued talking, "Do you really think this is something we should be talking about now?" she asked him, not really understanding where this was coming from. What was going on? Why was all this stuff coming at her like this? "I think I need to go," Tarilyn started to get up, but was stopped by Anthony grabbing her arm. "Please, don't go. I am sorry, I am being insensitive. Sit back down."

"Anthony."

"I apologized, come on. Don't I at least warrant some time? Let's order lunch. I am sure you haven't even eaten today." Tarilyn didn't want to sit down. She wanted to go and be with her family, but she felt so numb. Slowly she took her seat and glanced over the menu he handed her. She ordered fish and a sweet potato. While they ate,

Anthony made idle chatter, but Tarilyn's mind was a thousand miles away. Did he say he still wanted her? After all this time, why would he? She had tried not to think about it or him for that matter. She rarely dated in Atlanta, and it suited her fine. It wasn't that she didn't want to, she just poured herself into her job and taking care of Tion, so she didn't think of much else. Tarilyn didn't even realize Anthony was calling her name. "Earth to Tari, Earth to Tari," he chuckled as he waved his hands in front of her face.

"Oh, I am sorry."

"It's okay, but I would love to know what you were in such deep thought about," he inquired.

"You know there is something I need to tell you, and I am not sure you will want to speak to me afterwards."

"Oh really, and what is that?" he asked, becoming serious. Tarilyn watched him watch her, then she started to get nervous. She sighed and was about to speak when her phone started to ring. She placed one finger up as she saw her sister's name on the screen. "Hey, Tanisha," she said into the phone. She listened to her sister tell her they needed her at the funeral home in 30 minutes. She told her she would be there and ended the call. Covering her face

48

with her hands, it suddenly hit her again that her mother was gone. Suddenly without warning, Tarilyn began crying into her hands, and within seconds she felt Anthony's arms around her, consoling her. She tried not to let it register in her mind how good it felt. He handed her Kleenex and she cleaned her face. Excusing herself, she went to the ladies' room. She wiped her face off and looked in the mirror. She almost didn't recognize herself. When Tarilyn reached the table, Anthony stood up. "I… I need to get to the funeral home. They are waiting on me."

"Okay, are you alright though?"

"No, but I will be soon enough."

"Well you may need this. Your mother took care of mostly everything ahead of time, so just give this to the funeral director," Anthony said, reaching into his briefcase. Then, he handed her an envelope. It was similar to what she had already seen so she figured it was the copies. She took it from his hands, and he pulled her to him. Hugging her again, he kissed her forehead before releasing her. "You were going to tell me something before your call," he said to her.

Remembering what that was she felt uncomfortable, "Um, yeah. Do you mind if it waits? I really have to get going. I can call you later if that's okay."

"Yes, that's fine. Come on, I will head out with you," he placed money on the table to pay their bill and nodding to the waiter as he came over and cleared their table. They walked to the parking lot in silence. Anthony helped her in her car, and Tarilyn watched him walk to his before she waved and pulled off. Tarilyn drove in the direction of the funeral home, trying not to replay what happened during her time with Anthony. After about 10 minutes, Tarilyn pulled up to Swanson's Funeral Home. She turned the ignition off quickly, grabbed her purse, the envelope and headed inside. Opening the large white door, it was as if nothing had changed the last time she was here for her dad's arrangement. She noticed she was the first one there. Looking over to her left, she saw a group of people talking. They turned in her direction, and one of them walked in her path. She was greeted by their family friend, Mr. Earl, who was the director. "Tarilyn, look at you! Beautiful, just beautiful. Looking just like your mother. Speaking of that, I am so sorry to hear about her, but you know we will take care of everything."

"Thank you, Mr. Earl. I spoke with my mother's estate lawyer and he told me to give you this, it should take care of what my mother wanted. He said she had most of it planned and it was to be over with just as quickly," she told him, handing him over the package. As he took the package, the door opened and in walked her brothers and sister. They all followed Mr. Earl, as he took them into the parlor where they spent the next hour deciding on how to bury their mother. It was decided the services would be two days before Christmas. Once they were done, they all headed back to the house. Since Tanisha rode with her brothers, she asked Tarilyn if she could ride back with her instead. Waving to them, they got into the car and drove off. Tarilyn remembered she needed to call Tion. Tanisha tapped her arm and asked if they could talk before, she did that. Nodding, she glanced at her sister while they sat waiting for the light to turn green.

"So how are you holding up?"

"I guess about the same as you are. Although I did find out some things last night and today. I want to share them with you, but you have to promise me you won't say anything to Michael and Maurice."

"Okay, what's going on?"

"Well, mama was talking about a lot of stuff last night. She kept telling me I should tell Anthony and Tion about one another, and how she didn't want me to make the same mistakes she made when we were growing up."

"Really? Did she tell what she meant?"

"That's the thing, she didn't. So, when I pulled the paperwork, she told me about this morning, I came across a letter and a birth certificate."

Tarilyn reached into her purse quickly as the light, changed and handed both things to her sister, and let her read them as she continued to drive. Tarilyn couldn't see the expression on her sister's face as she watched the road. Turning on their street, she pulled up in front of the house and parked.

Tanisha's reaction was much like her own as she saw her hand go to her mouth, as the tears started. She turned to look over at Tarilyn and reached over and grabbed her hand. "No matter what you are always going to be my sister," Tanisha told her as she handed her back the papers. They sat in silence for a few minutes. Tarilyn was the first one to move, unbuckling her seat belt, and reaching for her purse.

"Come on, it's cold out here, let's go inside" Tarilyn told her as they got out and walked into the house.

They beat their brothers there as they headed into the den, Tanisha poured them glasses of wine, as they got cozy on the couch. Both sisters took a big gulp of the wine. Taking each other's hand as they were in the car, they continued the conversation, "Did you know mom hired Anthony to be her lawyer?"

"What? No, when did she do that?"

"According to him about four months ago."

"According to him? So, you've talked to him."

"Yes, we had lunch together today.

I was with him when you called," she told Tanisha as she proceeded to tell her all about her lunch with Anthony.

"Wow, sis. That's a lot to have to go through in one morning."

"Who are you telling? I am almost afraid to go to sleep tonight."

"Yeah. So, what are you going to do, are you going to try again with Anthony?"

"Honestly I haven't thought too much about it. Outside of me being overcome with all these sorts of new emotions, I don't know if Anthony fits into my life plans right now."

"What do you mean by that? Don't you think you deserve love?"

"Deserve it, yes but want it right it now in my life, I don't know. I haven't been with a man in almost six years."

"Six years?" Tanisha spat out her wine. She grabbed a towel as she looked at her sister sideways.

"Tarilyn what is wrong with you? How can you go that long without a man in your life?"

"I guess for the longest time, and even a little bit now I didn't feel pretty. Didn't even feel comfortable in my own skin. I would look down at my body and all I saw was flaws. So, if I didn't like myself, how could I expect anyone else to, especially a man?"

"Sis come here for a second," Tanisha stood up and then motioned for Tarilyn to do the same. Walking out of the den, Tanisha took Tarilyn by the hand and led her over to the bathroom. Hitting the light switch she stood her in front of the mirror and then stood behind her. "Look at you. I mean really look at you. You don't even wear full face makeup and look at how your skin is glowing. You are one of the most beautiful women I know. Don't ever doubt yourself. Beauty is skin deep. It's what's right here that makes you who you are. It's what's right here that will make any man, the luckiest person alive just to have you by his side," Tanisha told her as she had her hand over her sister's heart.

"You are one of the most genuine and kind-hearted persons I know. That right their accounts for everything, and even more, I love you."

"I love you too and I appreciate your words. I just need to start feeling them. I am almost there but sometimes it is still hard. I know I am good at my job, and I know I am a good mother. Deep down inside, I mean inside of all that, I still just see a work in progress," she hugged her sister and they went back out into the den. "So, are you going to tell Anthony about Tion?" Tanisha asked.

"Eventually but I really want to try and talk to Tion first."

"When will he be here?"

"Oh, shoot I still need to call him, but I made his flight arrangements for the morning."

"Oh okay, well let me let you call him. Then think about what you want to do for the rest of the day. I know we have to finish the rest of the prep for mama's funeral, but if you want to talk some more you know I am down."

"I have been up since 4 a.m. I feel like I need to rest but I don't want to lay down. I think I will go for a walk and call Tion, I will be back in a little while."

"Okay be careful," Tanisha told her as Tarilyn downed the rest of her wine.

Lost Love, Only love

Tarilyn didn't even know where she was going, but she needed a moment to herself to think. She again wondered why her mother thought she was strong enough to handle all this. Maybe this was her way of saying she needed to change her thinking as well. Tarilyn didn't know when she started looking at herself as a failure. Maybe it was because of how she thought Anthony was cheating. The whole situation just made her feel she wasn't enough of a woman for him. She always found a way to push men away afterwards. She used her work and being a mother as a crutch, and it wasn't until this moment that she saw that more than ever. Tarilyn could see her breath in a cloud of smoke, as she made her way up the street. She pulled her Bluetooth out of her pocket, placed it in her ear, and called her son. He answered after a few rings, "Hey mom. How are you?"

"Hey baby, I am okay, just trying to find some peace in this chaos. How did you do on your finals?"

"I did better than I thought I was going to, I got two A-'s and a B. I just finished packing."

"Tion, that is good, I am proud of you. Okay I will be there to get you from the airport when you land. The funeral is in a couple of days."

"Okay mom and thank you. You know that I get all my strength from you. You give me so much encouragement. I know I can do whatever I put my head and heart to." Tion told his mom. She was so glad he couldn't see her right now, as she wiped her half-frozen tears away.

"What did I do to deserve a son like you? Finish getting yourself together and I will see you in the morning, okay?"

"Okay mom, Love you."

"Love you too" she told him as she ended the call. Tarilyn hit the music button and sped up her walk. Before she realized it, she had walked into downtown Detroit. When she was younger, they would always walk straight down Grandriver instead of hopping the bus for the ride. Guess her mind knew where she wanted to go. Heading towards the ice-skating rink, she was excited to learn it was still there and open. Going over to the booth, she rented some skates and was on the ice in minutes. There were only a few other people there. She always loved to ice skate and missed that she couldn't do it in Atlanta as often. She skated until she was too tired to do it anymore. Sitting on the bench she watched the now crowded rink. There seemed to be a small class of young students enjoying themselves. She was getting ready to leave when someone sat next to her and handed her a cup of hot chocolate. Tarilyn turned her attention to the person, and was surprised to see it was Anthony, "How did you know I was done here?"

"Well I didn't, I just happened to be leaving my office and saw you out there skating. I see you're still as good as you were as a teen. I didn't know you still skated."

"I do when there is a rink available, "she told him, as she shivered. Taking a sip of the hot chocolate, and she closed her eyes as the warm of the liquid hit her insides. The taste wasn't even important as she continued to drink.

"Are you up for a drink and a little jazz? There is a spot that just opened about a year ago, I think you would love. I know the owner."

"Sure. Let me just send Tanisha a text so she won't be worried." Tarilyn didn't even notice that she had been gone and out on the rink for over two hours. They stood up and walked in the direction of the club he told her about.

Tarilyn was caught off guard when Anthony took her by the hand and intertwined their fingers. She was even more amazed at how the gesture made her blush. When they reached the building she looked up, the sign was flashing colors and read *My Jazzy Blues*. When they walked in, they were immediately greeted by an older gentleman. He turned to her and he looked at her strangely. The facial expression made Tarilyn feel uneasy, she shifted her weight to cut off the glare. The man cleared his throat and turned to greet Anthony, "Hey Rob. It's been a while."

"Hey Zeke, you know how they keep me busy. I would like you to meet Tarilyn. She is an old girlfriend. Actually, she is Darlene's daughter."

"Darlene? Darlene Johnston?"

"Yes, do you know my mother?" Tarilyn interrupted. Once again, he was glaring at her strangely. He mumbled something she didn't understand. She leaned in a little, "I am sorry, did you say something?"

"No. No. Yes, I knew your mother. We went to the same high school. I am sorry about your loss."

"Um… thank you," Tarilyn said. She looked over to Anthony, "Do you mind if we sit down? I am a little tired from the walking and skating."

"Oh sure. Okay Zeke, I will catch up with you later."

"I will send over some drinks, it's on me," Zeke said as he watched them walk away. Zeke walked over to the bar and poured him a drink, before he summoned one of his waitresses and sent her over to their table. Zeke literally had to catch his breath. He needed to focus and hoped he could divert his attention from them while they were there. Within a few minutes, his wish was granted as his normal happy hour crowd came in and kept him busy.

An hour into their time at the bar, the jazz band began to set up. Tarilyn made idle chat with Anthony as he questioned her about her home life. When the band finally started playing, they stopped talking and Tarilyn listened as the live jazz band created beautiful music. She was finally beginning to relax, and she was happy Anthony didn't try and continue their conversation while the band played. He must have been a regular there, as several people approached their table to speak with him. He took it all in stride, but it made her feel like they were back in college.

She felt what she was feeling back then… nonexistent. She decided not to focus on her thoughts, it wasn't as if they were dating or even a couple. Suddenly, as if he heard her thoughts, Anthony scooted up behind her and took her hand. She didn't say anything but kept listening to the music. When the band stopped for a thirty-minute break, she decided she was ready to go. "Anthony, it's been a long day, I am ready to go home. Do you mind ordering me a Lyft?"

"A Lyft? I can take you back to the house or the hotel Tari. It's not a big deal." She could tell he was offended by her question. She sighed heavily and nodded. She didn't have any energy for much else. She told him that she needed to go back to the house because that's where her car was. Anthony got the waitress' attention and asked for the bill. "Rob, it's been taken care of. It was nice meeting you Tarilyn. You both have a nice evening," she told them. Tarilyn looked over at Anthony, and he just shrugged his shoulders. He helped her up and they squeezed through the now extremely crowded club. On the way out the door, she felt someone was watching her. Looking up, she saw the owner. She nodded and smiled weakly, hurrying out the door. They walked a short block over to where Anthony's car was parked. Once they were settled into his car, he pulled out into traffic, "So I meant to ask you this earlier... How did the arrangements go?"

"They went. Your packet helped greatly, the services are on the 23rd, at my parents' church home."

"Okay, I will be there. I mean are you okay with me being there. I would like to be there for you and the rest of the family."

"I guess that's okay but why Anthony? Outside of your friendship with my mother that is."

"I meant what I said earlier. I have been thinking about us a lot lately and I would like us to get to know each other again."

"What if I am not that same little naïve girl you were with over 15 years ago? To be honest, she left the day we ended."

"I wasn't expecting you to be anyone but yourself. I want to know the person you are now. I could tell from the moment you walked into the lobby that you weren't that same person anymore."

"Anthony, accept my friendship for right now. That is all I can guarantee at this moment." Anthony turned onto her brother's street and pulled alongside her car. He placed his hands in his lap as he watched her tighten her coat. She reached for the door handle and Anthony grabbed her arm and turned her to him. Before she could react, he kissed her, and not just a peck. He kissed her with so much passion, she leaned more into the kiss as it deepened. After a few seconds, Tarilyn broke the kiss and she placed her hand on her mouth.

"Do your friends kiss you like that?" he asked her, giving her a look that she couldn't recognize. Without answering him, Tarilyn opened the car door and got into her car. Turning the ignition, she used that time to get her thoughts together. Why did he have to kiss her? *"Damn it,"* she thought as she realized she was out of breath. Her face felt flush, and she was mad at her body for reacting the way it did. She started to put her car in park but decided to text her sister that that she was outside and about to head back to the hotel. She waited until her sister responded before she got ready to drive off. Anthony was still waiting outside of her car. She waved and he pulled off. She headed down the street turning onto the main road heading back to the hotel. When she got up in her room, she ran bathwater.

64

She put her phone on the charger and noticed she had two messages from Anthony. The first said he made it home. The second said that he had missed her kiss. Setting the phone down, without responding, she got into the tub, closing her eyes. She replayed the kiss in her mind. What in the heck was she going to do? She wasn't sure she could give Anthony anything remotely close to what he wanted from her. She already knew what her mind state was. Did she want to go backwards with him? She sank further into the water. Why was he doing this to her? Wasn't she dealing with enough as it was? Maybe she wouldn't have to deal with it anyway. When she finally told him about Tion, he may never want to speak to her again. She definitely didn't need this. Tarilyn sat in the water until it was warm. She got out, turned the heat up, and lied down across the bed.

The next morning, once she woke up out of the dead sleep she had not even remember falling into, Tarilyn dressed and arrived at the airport 30 minutes early. She was surprised to see Tion waiting curbside for her. He opened the back door and put his suitcase on the seat. Leaning over, he kissed his mother. "Tion, why didn't you call me. How long have you been standing outside?" she scolded him slightly. "Not long. Our plane got in early, but I waited forever for the luggage. I was just about to call when I saw you pulling up," he told her. Tarilyn looked over at her son and smiled. "Are you doing okay? Are you going to tell me what happened with grams? I know you didn't want to tell me everything over the phone. But I am here now, and I want to know please." Her son pleaded with her. Just as his words spilled rapidly out his mouth, she saw the tears forming in his eyes. Tarilyn pulled over into the Denny's near the airport. Her son was right, he did deserve to know what was going on. He wasn't a little boy, he was a young man. When they were seated Tarilyn told Tion about her talk with her mother when she first arrived, and then she answered his questions that he had as she filled him in on everything else. Now came the hard part. She took a deep breath, grabbing his hands, she closed her eyes for a moment. She was scared of telling him, but he had a right to know, and it was now are never. "Ma. Why are you shaking. What's wrong?" Tion asked nervously.

"Tion, you remember when you were around seven and you asked me about your father? I promised you then that I would tell you when I thought you were ready. Well I think you are ready. Do you think you are ready to know about him now?" Tion looked at her and he looked about as scared as she did. He didn't say anything but asked if he could be excused for a few minutes. She nodded. She took the time to get her words together. She only hoped Tion and Anthony understood her reasons. Within a short time, Tion sat back down. She could tell he was still a little shaken up. Now she was about to shake him up even more.

"Ma, why now?"

"Because I promised your grandmother and I never want you to feel as if I kept you from him. It was never my real intent. It just happened that way, but you deserve to have him in your life if you choose to," Tarilyn told her son. He nodded and listened as she explained to him about her relationship with Anthony. "I never told him about you, because I didn't want him to feel obligated to do the right thing. Essentially, our time together played its course. I didn't blame him for that, I always felt I was an average girl. He was the star basketball player in high school and in college. I didn't find out I was pregnant with you until after graduation, and then I moved to Atlanta. I avoided the calls because I felt guilty. So, I hadn't seen or talked to him since then... until yesterday."

"So, you never even told him about me. Mom, why did you think so little about yourself back then? I mean you are so pretty and smart. Doesn't that count for anything?"

"It should but it's a little hard to explain. I just never thought I measured up. From the first day you came into this world, I knew the one thing I would be good at is being your mother, and that is what I focused on. I hope you can forgive me for being a little selfish when it came to you."

"I think I understand, but I am glad you finally talked to me about this. You gave me such a good childhood, I never gave it too much thought, but I will meet him, if that's okay with you."

"Yes Tion, that's fine with me, but son, he still doesn't know about you. He knows I have a son, but that's all he knows. We were interrupted when I tried to tell him. So, I am not sure how this is going to go, and I don't want you hurt, if for any reason he doesn't want to be a part of your life." Tion nodded and wiped a tear from his face. Looking at his tear stained face, Tarilyn hoped she was making the right decision. After a few seconds, Tion looked over at her. He seemed hesitant but then spoke, "Do you have a picture of him?"

"I have this," she told him as she reached into her purse and then handed him the business card which had his picture on it. Tion studied the card. He could see he had some of the same features as his father. Immediately he felt it in his gut, he wanted to meet him. He just hoped his father would be open to meeting him as well. He sighed and handed the card back to his mother, he didn't want to give it anymore thought.

"Are you okay?"

"Yeah, I mean I will be."

"Finish your food so we can get out of here, your cousins are waiting on you."

"I'm good. I don't have much of an appetite anymore."

"You sure, Tion?"

"Yes ma'am."

"Okay," she responded. As she got up to pay the bill, Tion went ahead to the car. He was silent the rest of the way to the house. She really hoped keeping this holiday promise was not more than they could all handle. Glancing up to the sky and saying a silent prayer to her mom, they headed into the house. They were greeted with screams and hugs from his cousins and Tion was whisked away. Tarilyn threw her purse on the table and sat across from her sister who was sitting at the dining room table drinking her coffee.

"What's wrong?"

"I don't know how much of a good idea this is."

"What is? Are you talking about what we talked about yesterday?

"Yes, I told him at breakfast and Tion isn't mad which I am grateful of but, I think he is now afraid if he will be accepted if they meet."

"Listen Tari, you are making the right decision, now you have to tell Anthony and let the chips fall where they may."

"You make is sound so simple."

"Well it definitely isn't that but at the same time. You don't want to have this hanging over your head the rest of your life, like it seems that mom did."

"Tanisha, this is tearing me up. The look on his face I would never want to see again."

"Tari, I know, I know. Let's just not talk about this anymore and try and get through these next couple of days." Tarilyn just nodded. They set at the table in silence, listening to the older kids talk. She was glad to hear Tion laughing and joking with his cousins. The rest of the day was spent working on the funeral as other family members dropped by with food and memories. Tarilyn had not touched her phone on purpose and wasn't surprised when she saw a couple of messages from Anthony.

Hey Tari. I just wanted to check in on you and make sure that you were doing okay, you need anything?

Well it's been awhile, and I haven't heard back, if you are up for talking or a visit, call or text me. Talk to you soon.

Tari sighed, as she typed on the screen, "*Sorry I just saw these, the day has been filled with family. I am doing okay but will probably be here helping out for the rest of the night, ttyl.*"

I'm A Father?

Tarilyn just wanted to keep it short and sweet but overall, she wasn't sure what she really should have wrote. Based on the things he said the day before she was unsure of them being able to be friends. She got ready to stand up when she heard the doorbell. She walked over to the door assuming it was just more family stopping by. Opening the door, she was surprised to see to Anthony at the door.

"Anthony, what... what are you doing here?"

"Well I knew if asked if I could stop by you would nix the idea."

"So, you just thought it was okay to just stop by?" she asked him, trying not to let it upset her. Michael walked by and looked out the door. "Hey Ant! How you doing? It's been a minute. Come on in, Maurice's in the other room and so is Dex." Her brother rattled off as if she wasn't even standing there.

"Dex? Ah man, I have to go and speak."

"Come on man." Michael told him, and Tarilyn just stepped back and walked off, pissed as she headed into the kitchen, she heard Michael close the front door, and then the room erupted in conversation. All she could hear was

72

the guys talking and laughing. Reaching for a glass, she grabbed the open wine bottle and poured the rest of the liquid in her glass. Sipping it, she was just about to go and look for her sister when Tion walked up behind her, startling her.

"Ma?"

"Tion, you scared me, why aren't you upstairs with the rest of the kids?"

"I just wanted to get something to eat, is it okay if I go in there and grab me something?"

"Sure, oh shoot wait, Tion. Anthony just walked in."

"My dad?"

"Yes…" Tarilyn started to explain more to Tion when they were caught off guard but the male's voice, they heard behind them, turning they were both looking at Anthony who had an expression that Tarilyn couldn't decipher. "Dad? What does he mean by 'my dad'?" Anthony said looking at the young man who very well could have been him back in high school. Quickly getting out of his thoughts he waited for Tarilyn to answer, as he walked into the kitchen area and closer to Tion. Tarilyn was immediately flustered and she wanted to disappear. Sighing, she put her glass back on the table and grabbed Tion's hand. He looked terrified and confused. She squeezed his hand to reassure him as she gave her full attention to Anthony.

"I'm… I'm sorry. I didn't want you to find out like this. This is my son Tion, I mean our son Tion."

"Tion… I feel like I am looking in a mirror. You have to be what… almost 17 right?" he asked, as he extended his hand. Tion nodded yes. He looked at his mother for a second, then back to Anthony before he dropped his mother's hand and reached out to shake Anthony's hand. Within half a second, Tion was in Anthony's arms. Tarilyn stood there, willing her tears not to start as she kept one hand over her mouth and another on her chest. Her heart was beating fast as the scene continued in front of her. Hearing footsteps, she looked over as Tanisha walked into the kitchen just as they released. Her eyes and mouth were wide open. "Oh shit," Tanisha said as she scooted next to Tarilyn so that she wouldn't interrupt the moment.

"So, you aren't mad at mom about me?"

"I wouldn't exactly say that, more shocked than anything, but I know there has to be a reason she kept you from me for seventeen years, and with everything that is going on, I won't ask what that is today."

"Yes, there was, and thank you for not blowing up at me at this moment."

"We will talk before I leave. I almost forgot the originally reason I came in here, Maurice sent me in here for a glass," he told her as Tion stepped around his mother, retrieving the glass and handing it to Anthony. The room fell silent all at once, and it seemed everyone was waiting for a reaction from the next. Suddenly Tion's stomach growled and he turned a shade darker. Smiling uneasily, Tarilyn pat him on the arm, "Go in there and get you something to eat please then go on back upstairs, okay?" He walked out without saying anything else. Anthony whistled low and mumbled something that both sisters couldn't hear. What Tarilyn could notice was the sudden look of hurt on his face.

You Are My Family

Tarilyn willed herself not to reach out to Anthony and touch his face or shoulder, she wanted to erase that hurt. Anthony looked at her and then down to the glass he was holding.

"Let me go take this in the other room, I'll catch up with you in a few."

"Okay." Tarilyn replied as they watched him walk out. Tanisha turned and looked her sister directly in the face. "Girl what the hell are you going to do now?" Not knowing how to answer, Tarilyn picked up her glass and downed the wine in one big gulp, "Is there anymore wine?" Tanisha chuckled, shaking her head at her sister, as she pulled another bottle out of the cabinet to their left. Tanisha waved for her to follow her to the den. Instead of sitting, Tarilyn began pacing. Tanisha tapped on her leg when she had walked past her for the fourth time.

"Can you please sit down? You are making me dizzy."

"I can't. I feel ... Ugh I don't know how I am feeling, I don't want to hurt either of them, but I guess it is kind of too late to think that of that huh."

"Uh yea, but don't worry about it. You have just as much on your plate to think about as they do, at this point they are either going to forge a relationship or not."

"You make it seem so easy."

"Tari, Tion is seventeen years old, a senior in high school. It may not be easy but realistically it's not that hard. Anthony and Tion are the only two that can decide what happens past this day and no matter how you may want it to go."

"I guess you are right, but do you wonder why he wasn't mad like Tion mentioned? Do you think maybe mama prepared him for this, told him a little something?"

"Tari! Now why would you think something like that?"

"Shit, shit, shit. I don't know." Tarilyn said, as she plopped down on the couch next to Tanisha, placing her face in her hands. She willed the tears not to start. One thing that kept crossing her mind was if she ruined her relationship with Tion. It was the one thing that mattered more to her than anything. Tanisha grabbed the glass from the table and picked up the bottle of wine. She refilled her glass first and then Tarilyn's. Once again, Tarilyn emptied the glass with one gulp and Tanisha laughed at her.

"Come on Tari seriously, we have enough to do and think about for the next couple of days. Yeah, this didn't happen the way you may have wanted it to but trust me, it happened way calmer than it could have."

"I guess you are right about that," Tarilyn said after sighing. She knew her sister was right, so she pushed the scene out of her head, while Tanisha pulled out the notebook and they started working on their mother's obituary. Tanisha started writing as Tarilyn asked questions about the obituary. It took them nearly an hour. Tarilyn had just gotten up when she heard someone clear their throat. Tarilyn and Tanisha looked over to Tion and Anthony standing in the room. Tarilyn wasn't sure what expression was on her face, but it immediately felt hot. Finding her voice, "Wha... What's going on?" she stuttered out. Tion moved closer to her and looked back at Anthony.

"Is it okay if I go take a ride with my dad?"

"A ride?"

"Yes. I asked him if we could talk and he suggested the ride, since it's so many people here in support of grandma."

"I guess I don't mind. You won't keep him out, late will you?" Tarilyn directed her question to Anthony, who gave her a half smile.

"No, I won't keep him out late, you have my word."

"Okay, well just be careful. Tion can you just text me when you are on your way back. I might head back to the hotel, and Anthony can drop you off there."

"Okay Ma," Tion said as he leaned over and kissed her. Anthony winked and mouthed, "Thank you," as they turned and walked out the den side by side. Tarilyn watched them until she heard the front door close. She gave her sister a look before she opened the box of pictures. Now she really needed to get her mind on other things. Tanisha touched her arm. Tarilyn looked up at her sister. "Are you okay with what just happened?"

"I don't know, but do I really have a choice?'

"Well not really. It will all work out, just let the chips fall where they may at this point," Tanisha told her and Tarilyn nodded. Picking up her glass, she took a sip as her sister split the pictures with her and they started going through them in silence. One by one, Tarilyn looked through the pictures placing the ones she wanted to the side. She thought of how much she loved her family as she smiled and looked at the pictures. She was almost done when one caught her eye. Tarilyn ran her hand over the picture of her mother Tara and a man, they looked so in love. She brought the picture closer to her face when it hit her. She had seen the man before, but he was older. The man in the picture was the owner of the club Anthony took her to a couple days ago… was he her father? She showed the picture to Tanisha. "Sis, do you know who the man in this picture is with my mother?" Tanisha took the picture and nodded, "Yes. That was her boyfriend back then, I remember him a little bit."

"Is he my father?"

"Has to be, Auntie Tara was never with any other man than him. I don't remember his name though."

"Remember it was on the birth certificate? It said Darnell Wilkinson."

"Darnell right, I recall now."

"I met him," Tarilyn said as she picked the picture up and staring at it again, then placing the picture into her purse.

"What? What do you mean you met him?"

"Yeah, the other day when I was out with Anthony, he introduced me. I noticed he looked at me strangely, but I thought nothing of it."

"Wow, I thought he didn't live here anymore," Tanisha told her as she handed over another stack of pictures. Tarilyn was about to say something else when Michael stepped into the den.

"Are y'all almost done with the stuff for the obituary? I want to make sure I have everything to take to the printer in the morning."

"Yeah, we are almost done. Just want to tweak the writings we all did and then we are all set. I will make sure to leave it on the table for you," Tanisha told him. Michael looked over at Tarilyn and had a strange look on his face. "Tari, why are you crying?" Wiping her face, Tarilyn had not even realized she was crying until he said something. "Is this about Anthony?"

"Anthony?"

81

"Yeah seeing him and everything?"

"No... no that's not it. Can you go get Maurice? I have something to show you both," Tarilyn said and she grabbed some Kleenex from the back table. Tanisha grabbed Tarilyn's hands, squeezing them until her brothers returned. Tarilyn hadn't given much thought to when she was going to tell them, but now was as good a time as any. This evening hadn't turned out like she had thought it would, but then again what was she expecting it to be? After a few minutes, she heard her brothers letting the rest of the relatives out as they came into the den. It was after 10:00 and it was getting late. They had one more day until the services. Maurice and Michael came into the room and sat down. Reaching into her purse Tarilyn handed Michael her birth certificate. He read it and his eyes widened as he handed it to Maurice. "This doesn't change anything, you know, that right?" Maurice told her as he laid the document on the table.

"Right, you are our sister and always will be." Michael said as he stood, pulled Tarilyn up, and hugged her. The tears started again. She was glad her brothers didn't let the news change anything, but she just wanted them to know. They were family, and now they needed to stand together even more. "Can we please keep this between us though? I don't want the kids to know, and if possible, your wives too. I just don't want to be pushed into more questions. I don't even plan on telling Tion." They all nodded in agreement to her request and she sighed.

"Speaking of Tion, so he and Anthony know about each other now huh?" Michael asked.

"Yeah, they do… not exactly how I planned on revealing it, but it happened. I still don't know how to feel about it. This has all just been so much."

"I am sure it has been. Anthony seems pretty cool with it, like he was sort of prepared for it or something."

"Funny Mikey, I thought the exact same thing. For some reason I think mama had some play in that but it's something I am going to ask him tomorrow when we talk but you know what? I am drained. I think I am going to head back to the hotel and see you guys tomorrow, okay?"

"Okay sis, we will see you in the morning. 11:00 right?" Maurice asked before kissing her on the forehead and heading up the back stairs to his room. Michael started cleaning up and gave her another hug. Tarilyn looked over to her sister who was texting. "Do you need a ride?"

"No, my friend is on his way to come and get me. I need a harder drink than this wine."

"Understood, see you later and be careful," Tarilyn told her as she went to the coat closet and retrieved her coat and grabbed her purse. She opened the door and ran smack into Tion.

"Tion, you scared me."

"Sorry ma. I guess we had good timing," he said, stepping in and attempting to close the door. Tarilyn held onto it.

"Yeah, so are you staying here, or coming back with me?"

"With you, but I need to run upstairs for my backpack."

"Okay I will meet you in the car." Tarilyn told him as she opened the door. She walked down the front steps and got into her car. Sitting behind the wheel, she heard her phone go off. Reaching for it in her purse, she guessed it was probably Anthony. Looking at the screen, she read his message: *Although I have a lot of unanswered questions, I just wanted to say thank you.* Tarilyn typed back to him: *Thank you? I am a bit surprised at that but can understand*

the unanswered questions. Do you want to meet for
breakfast?

I can't. I have an early morning meeting. How
about lunch or dinner? I know you may have a lot to do
tomorrow.

Early lunch if possible. We are meeting to finalize
everything around 2:00 and then pick out mom's outfit.

Okay I will text you as soon as I have an idea of
what time. Good night.

Goodnight Anthony.

Tarilyn put her phone down when Tion opened the
car door. She was surprised to see Anthony pull off, he was
parked a few cars in front of them. She had not even looked
around when she walked to her car. She wasn't sure if she
should ask how Tion and Anthony's talk went. Then she
decided she would let him bring it up. The short drive to
the hotel was quiet. They just listened to the music. It
made her worry. Was he upset with her now or when she
first told him? Reaching over she touched his hand as she
was parking. "Are you okay Tion?"

"Huh? Oh yeah I am, I will tell you about it after
my shower." Tion told her as he got out the car and

grabbed his things. Tarilyn nodded. She watched him for a few minutes before she got out the car, and they headed inside the hotel. She showered first and then went into the sitting area to watch TV. Their room had a kitchen, so she decided to make tea while she waited for Tion. She was on pins and needles not knowing what he was going to share with her. It had been almost an hour when Tion finally walked into the sitting room. He sat across from her and looked as if he didn't know what to say.

"So, Ma, the talk with Anthony, I mean my dad was very interesting. I learned some things about who he was when you two were together up until now. He showed me pictures of you and him together in high school and college. You two looked so happy back then."

"We were actually. He just let his basketball stardom get to his head and the way my self-esteem was back then I just couldn't handle it. I owe you and him an apology though, I wasn't fair to either of you. I truly apologize Tion, but back then I didn't want to take that chance on him not wanting you because of the attention he was getting. I knew he had gotten drafted by a team, and I would have been either holding him back or facing rejection. I chose not to say anything instead." Tarilyn explained to her son, he opened his mouth and then closed it. She could see that he had so many other questions that he wanted to ask. Finally, he spoke…

"Can I ask you something?"

"Sure, anything."

"Did you feel like you weren't pretty back then because of your weight?"

"Yes, I felt that way until I just lost the weight. I felt I was blessed to have you, and for me you were all I needed, that's why I never dated seriously. When I was younger, your auntie Nisha had all the guys around her, and I was always the one the guys could just hang with and study with. That was until I met Anthony. He made me feel like I was the only woman in the world, and I hung on to that. He never treated me mean or anything, and it was what made me fall for him overall. Did I love your father? Yes, and a part of me has never stopped."

"Ma, I am so sorry that you grew up feeling like that."

"Don't be, it was a long time ago. I've always had to work on my self-esteem. It was always a huge reason why I always showed confidence in you, and gave you so much encouragement," she told him, and Tion got up and gave her a hug. "I love you mom."

"I love you back son, for always. I hope this won't put a strain on our relationship."

"No, it won't, we are good. I understand that you were doing things you thought were for the best for me."

"How did I get so lucky?"

"I should be asking myself that. Now I have two parents, I am more than lucky. I am going to head to bed now, see you in a few hours," Tion said, as he released her and went to bed. Tarilyn sat and thought about the conversation they just had. She told her son things that she thought that she would never have to share with him, and that hurt her more than she ever would admit.

Your Mirror Don't See What I See

Tarilyn sipped her now cold tea and she closed her eyes while the picture of her parents came into her mind. Would she approach Darnell Wilkinson? She wasn't sure if she wanted to. Her head started hurting and she felt she needed to lie down. Finishing the tea, she placed the cup into the sink and headed back into her room. Glancing at her phone she saw she had a text message. She picked up her phone and began to read.

Anthony: I can't stop thinking about all this. I can't believe I have a son! A huge part of me wants to be mad at you, but I can't. I know we will talk about this tomorrow but why didn't you tell me? Why?

Tarilyn: I don't know. I would rather tell you what I told Tion in person. I know you have a right to feel the way you do, and I won't take that from you, in fact you both do. I just don't want to do it this way, please. I'll see you tomorrow. Good night Anthony.

Tarilyn immediately felt numb, she willed the tears not to fall again. She already knew she wouldn't be getting any sleep. She pulled on pants, a sweater, and shoes. Walking over to the patio door she stepped out and sat in the chair. Listening to the night sounds downtown, she wrapped her arms around herself. There wasn't a breeze, but it was still cold out. Tarilyn didn't care, it was helping to clear her mind. Freezing her thoughts, she argued with herself as she watched the light snow flakes that started to fall. She stayed outside for about an hour until she was almost frozen. She went back inside to warm up more tea and was surprised to see Tion sitting at the table.

"What are you doing up?"

"I couldn't sleep, so I decided to eat the leftovers I brought from grams house."

"Oh okay. Tion, I really am sorry I have shaken up your world. I know losing your grandmother was enough, and to add all this just wasn't fair."

"Ma, I know you did what you thought was best. It is a lot to take in. I was just lost in my thoughts, thinking how I wouldn't have any more weekend calls from her, how she used to encourage me with our talks. I don't know how I am going to get used to not having that," Tion told her through tears. Tarilyn pulled him into a hug and he cried harder. Tion was close to his grandmother. He spent at least two weeks here a summer, then came back to Atlanta to work for the summer. Tarilyn knew there was nothing she could say to change the hurt he was feeling, holding him was all she could manage to do. She held him until his tears subsided. He got up and got a Kleenex, before they went into the sitting area. Turning on the television, they sat on the couch next to each other. They partially watched the movie, in their own thoughts. Tion fell asleep first. Tarilyn kissed his forehead lightly as she tried to actually watch the movie. She failed. The next couple of days were going to hit her, she knew it. The same thing happened with her dad. Closing her eyes, her mother immediately came into her vision. Tarilyn thought back to her mother sitting on the bed when Tarilyn walked in, and how she was reading her Bible. The things her mother said and made Tarilyn promise came flooding back once again. Now it all made sense.

Tarilyn begin to wring her hands, a habit she thought she surpassed when she lost her weight. Suddenly her phone began to vibrate. She turned it over and saw it was the one person she wasn't trying to let enter her thoughts. Did she want to talk to him now? She answered but paused before saying anything. They sat in silence for a few seconds, and then he spoke.

"Hello?"

"Yes, I am here. How are you Anthony?"

"I am doing okay. I didn't wake you, did I?"

"No. You are good, what's up?" she asked him. She shifted her leg and standing up stood so she wouldn't disturb Tion sleeping. Glancing at the clock near the television she was surprised. It was 4:37 a.m., what was he doing up? "I just noticed the time, what are you doing up?"

"I don't know, I just couldn't stop thinking about the last three days. My life has changed hugely in that short time frame."

"I apologized to Tion earlier. I know that I owe you an apology as well," she started but quickly closed her mouth when Anthony cut her off.

"Apology? What's the apology for?"

"For keeping Tion from you."

"Well in all honesty we are both at fault. I never once tried to reach out to you and see how you were, why you left, anything. I just let it all go because of my impending career. In the end I lost way more," he said. Tarilyn didn't know how to respond. She didn't see it that way, but she wasn't going to push.

"Are you still there?"

"Yes, I was just listening to what you said. Okay so we are both at fault. The big question is how, would you like to go about this from here? As far as seeing Tion once we go back to Atlanta?"

"I'm still thinking on that, but let's talk about that after the services. Today is the body viewing. Are you ready?"

"Not even a little bit but she is out of pain and free. So, I and we will get through this together, that's the most important thing."

"Yea you are right. I won't hold you on this phone. I just needed to hear your voice for a few minutes. I will see you in a few hours, good night."

"Good night Anthony." Tarilyn walked into her bedroom as they were talking. She put her phone down on her nightstand and continued to watch the big flakes hit the balcony patio. This was something that she didn't miss about home, and that was the weather. Especially the snow. She diverted her attention from the snow back to the conversation she just had. Co-parent… that was something she never thought that she would have to do with Tion. She didn't see them in this situation. Grabbing her covers she pulled them back. She sat down and pulled herself into the bed, sleep was starting to take over. She didn't fight it as she closed her eyes and slept.

Tarilyn was awakened by soft pushes. She wasn't sure if she was dreaming or not, but she felt groggy as hell, as she attempted to fully open her eyes and focus. She heard Tion's voice. "Ma. Ma.?"

"Yes, I'm woke. What's wrong?"

"Nothing we are just running behind, I guess we both overslept." He told her as she finally got her vision and thoughts straight. He was fully dressed.

"What time is it?"

"Almost ten- thirty."

"Okay call your auntie and let her know we are leaving out and will meet them at the funeral home. I'll be ready in fifteen. Tarilyn waited until Tion walked out of the room before she threw the covers off her and slowly pulled her tired body from the bed, turning the shower on she quickly got her clothes ready as well as her mind for the day. The body viewing was today. Six hours, she hoped she would be able to make it through this whole day. It took her twenty minutes to get ready, Tion was waiting for her patiently, she wished she could take away the pain she saw in his eyes.

"Ready. Were you able to reach your auntie?"

"Yes, she said okay."

"Are you hungry? We can stop on the way."

"Yes please."

"Okay, let's get out this door. We will get through this today. We will." She told him as she herself held her tears from falling. Tarilyn and Tion were heading through the lobby when Tion tapped her on the arm and pointed to Anthony sitting in a lobby chair. He stood up and smiled slightly as they walked in his direction. "Good morning, what are you doing here? I thought I wouldn't see you until later?"

"Yeah, I decided that maybe I would be your driver for the day, give you both some extra time to prepare for the next few days."

"Thanks Dad, that was nice of you. Is it okay if I call you that?"

"Dad, wow. I like the sound of that," Anthony said, putting his arm around Tion. They all headed towards the door. Tarilyn let them walk ahead of her. She watched as they talked, she was pleased to see they were both trying. Anthony opened the car door for her and there were purple roses sitting on the seat. She held them as she sat down. Purple roses were always her favorite, Anthony remembered. She inhaled their scent as he walked around. Anthony looked at her when he got in. "Thank you," she told him, as she took him by the hand and squeezed. Anthony pulled out of the lot and they headed towards the funeral home. Tarilyn kept silent as she listened to them talk about Tion's football career at school. She couldn't help but smile, she never expected this union to go this way. Did she have her mother to attribute for it? Anthony pulled up to the front of the funeral home, and suddenly Tarilyn's stomach rumbled.

"Sounds like someone is hungry."

"Yeah. Sorry we were intending on stopping on the way here."

"How about you go ahead in? I saw your family pull up, I'll go and grab something to eat for you and Tion."

"Are you sure? I don't want to take you out of your way."

"I insist."

"Okay, thank you. Tion knows what I eat from wherever you stop at."

"Yea, she is pretty much a stickler for her what she eats," Tion said from the back. Anthony laughed.

"Okay we will be back soon." Anthony told her as she got out the car. He held the door for Tion as he got in the front seat.

The Surprises Just Keep On Coming

Turning, Tarilyn headed to the funeral home front entrance and was greeted by Tanisha.

"Good afternoon Sis. Was that Anthony?"

"Yeah, he came by the hotel and volunteered to be our chauffeur for the rest of the day."

"Wow, isn't that nice of him?" Tanisha said as they were greeted by the receptionist. Tanisha gave her the name of the representative who was waiting on them. The brothers walked in shortly after. They all made small talk until the representative came out to get them. The next hour was spent going over the final arrangements for their mother. Tarilyn sat numb as she half listened to the things that had been set up for their mother. When the representative was done, he set a piece of paper in front of Tarilyn, and the room got quiet.

"What's this?" she asked, glancing over the paper. She could feel her siblings watching her. The paper was the final cost of the arrangements. He told them, there were some extra items that weren't included in the proposed balance their mother had paid. Tarilyn finally looked down at the bottom and her mouth fell open when she noticed that there was no balance. It had already been paid.

They all knew her policy had covered most of it, but Tari planned on paying the balance herself. Michael reached over and took the paper from her. Confused, Tarilyn looked at the funeral representative. "Who paid the balance?" she asked him.

"I did," a voice said from behind them. They all turned, and Tari was shocked to see the man whom she met at the bar the other night. Michael and Maurice both stood up and walked over to him, extending their hands in greeting.

"Why did you pay it?"

"It was the least I could do, I owed Darlene a lot. I am still in shock that she is gone. I hope I haven't offended anyone by doing this," he said, as he walked more into the room.

"No, no it's okay. Isn't it Tari?" Tanisha commented, grabbing her sister by the hand. They knew who he was, Tari had yet to say anything. She looked at him up and down, squinting her eyes and analyzing him. *"Did she have some of his features, his ways?"* she thought to herself. Tanisha gently nudged her when she still hadn't responded. "Oh yeah, yes it's okay. Thank you."

"Before the viewing starts, can I talk to you for a few minutes?"

"Sure… Zeke, right?'

"Darnell, I would rather you call me… that" he told her, as he paused briefly.

"Oh, okay Darnell Let me wrap up here first, I will meet you up front," she told him, as she turned back to her sister. Tanisha had a strange look on her face.

"What's that about? What does he need to talk to you about?" Michael asked.

"Yeah, why does he want to talk to you?" Maurice interjected.

"Not sure, but I will be sure to update you both later." The representative who walked back in, he pointed into the area where their mother laid for the last time. Taking a deep breath, Tarilyn grabbed her sister's hand and they all followed.

Entering the large room, they all walked to the front slowly. Her brothers walked closer together. Maurice shoulders shook hard and she could hear him crying. Michael's face was focused as if he was seeing through the whole setup. He didn't have any emotion, he was the same way with their dad.

Tarilyn and Tanisha continued to inch their way down the walkway. Tarilyn could see her mother lying there and instantly her knees felt weak. Taking two deep breaths, she tried to calm herself as she closed her eyes briefly. The tears formed as soon as she did. Seeing their mother Tarilyn felt like her heart was crumbling into pieces. She wasn't ready for this, she felt like she was about to hyperventilate. Stopping, she released Tanisha. "I... I am sorry. I can't walk up there just yet," she mumbled, shaking. Tanisha's eyes were red with tears, but she nodded and continued walking towards the casket. Michael came and stood next to her when she finally reached it. Touching the casket, Tanisha began humming like their mother used to do to calm them. Tanisha cried harder, almost collapsing to the floor, as Michael tried to hold on to her. The visual almost made Tari run out but she decided to take a seat on the side.

She didn't hear Tion and Anthony come in. Tion touched her shoulder and she nearly jumped out her skin. He leaned over and kissed her, slightly pulling her up. She still wasn't ready, but she couldn't tell her son that. They reached the casket when Tarilyn tightened her grip on Tion's hand. Her tears flowed instantly. She almost didn't recognize her mother. She looked so peaceful, it was the first time Tarilyn saw her that calm in a long time. It made her feel better, but it still hurt that she would not hear her voice anymore. She pulled Tion closer to her after a few minutes. He was sobbing hard. "I didn't get to say goodbye," he whispered, touching her face slightly. He cried harder. Anthony came up behind them both and took control of Tion. Michael came over and led Tarilyn away from the room. It was too much for all of Tarilyn's siblings, even if they didn't show it like she did. She felt it. Grabbing Kleenex, she cleaned her face as they walked towards the lobby. The viewing was in the next hour. She needed some air before they started greeting family and friends.

Tarilyn walked down the hallway without paying attention to her surroundings. When she made it the lobby, she almost ran straight into Darnell.

"Whoa! Where are you running off to?"

"Oh, I am sorry, I was trying to get some air for a minute."

"Okay, okay. Can I join you so we can still talk?" he asked.

"Yeah that's fine, come on," she responded, as they walked out the door together. Neither one of them saw Anthony had been watching them.

Darnell led Tari over to a bench and took her by the hand. Tarilyn looked up at him and studied his features again. She saw his mouth moving but her mind wasn't letting her register what he was saying, "Tari, Tari?" he called her named, repeatedly. Blinking her eyes, she blushed slightly in embarrassment as she focused on what he was saying. "I'm sorry... what did you say?"

"Wow... never in my life did I think I would be seeing a complete replica of the love of my life, in front of me again." Darnell said softly.

"Can you tell me about her?"

"I sure can, I can spend all day doing that. That's part of the reason I wanted to talk to you. When I left you in the care of Darlene, I just couldn't handle seeing you. You were growing up looking so much like Tara. I mean everything about her, her smile, laughter, and it just hurt me to my core. She was my everything," he said. Pulling out his wallet he took out a folded, tattered picture and handed it to her. Tarilyn thought she was looking at herself. "That was Tara when she was sixteen, right when she got pregnant with you."

"That's my mother?" She looked so different than the other pictures she had seen of her. Her mother was always in the background, off to the side. Now that Tarilyn thought about it, so was she.

"Yes, it is." Handing the picture back to him, a lot of things were making sense but were also even more overwhelming. Why didn't her mother tell her all this?

"Listen, I don't want to upset you even more. Let's do dinner in a couple days and talk. I would like to take your son too."

"Okay, that's fine. I look forward to it, but let's get back in here people are going to start showing up soon and I need to get myself together."

"Okay baby girl, thank you for giving me this little time with you. I haven't been able to function much since you came into the bar that day with Anthony." He squeezed her hand and let it go. They stood up and headed back inside. She knew that night his response was off, now she knew why.

   Anthony watched Tarilyn and Darnell. He couldn't hear their conversation. His mind was going crazy wondering what they spoke about. He did notice the look Darnell gave Tarilyn when they were introduced a few days ago, but he let it just go by. Darnell was old enough to be her father he thought... her father? Could that, be it? Shaking his head, he let the thought leave his mind as quickly as it entered. He wasn't going to think about it, but he would ask what was going on after all this was over. Then he wondered if he had a right to interfere and ask anything. Tarilyn wasn't his woman, as much as he wanted that opportunity again. Anthony felt she just wasn't interested. He was the one who did the damage to them. Glancing down at his watch, he decided to leave. He would come back later and check on her and Tion, but he didn't want to leave without saying anything. He was about to move when he heard his name being called. Turning, he was surprised to see Bridget, his soon to be ex-wife. "Bridget? What are you doing here?" he asked, as she walked closer. He wasn't a bit shocked with what she had on: a low-cut blouse that showed her breasts, and a tight, almost mini.

"I was just about to ask you the same thing," she told him. She placed her arms around his neck, leaning in as if she wanted him to take the bait and kiss her. He tried to stop her but was too late as Bridget's lips hit his. The feeling in his stomach felt heavy. He quickly pulled away when he heard someone clearing their throat. His eyes got large when he saw the look on Tion's face. He was just about to say something when Tarilyn and Darnell both walked in. Anthony took Bridget's arms from his neck and wiped her lipstick off his mouth, hoping Tari didn't see.

"Dad… who is this?" Tion finally asked. Anthony started to answer when he was interrupted. "Yes Anthony, who's your lady friend?" Tarilyn asked with hurt and confusion on her face. Anthony didn't know what to do, he didn't hear them come in or see Tion enter the lobby. He was truly stuck. The last thing Tarilyn and Tion needed was seeing this. Smiling sweetly, Bridget turned towards Tarilyn extending her hand, "My name is Bridget, I'm Anthony's wife."

"Excuse me, did you say wife?" Tarilyn replied with a frown. She completely ignored Bridget's extended hand. Bridget put her hand down as if it didn't matter to her one way or the other.

Tarilyn immediately thought back to all of their conversations and tried to remember if he said he was single. One thing was for sure, he wasn't wearing a ring, nor did he have the markings of one. Tarilyn took a deep breath as she waited for one of them to reply. Before they could say anything, Darnell jumped in. "Bridget, what are you doing here? Don't come in starting no unnecessary mess."

"Mess? Me? Now you know…" she started but was stopped by Anthony.

"Bridget let's step outside." Turning to Tion he said, "Son I will be right back." Taking Bridget by the arm he led her out of the funeral home. Tion walked over to his mother and Darnell.

"Tion, this is Darnell. He wants to take us to dinner after the funeral is over and so we can all talk."

"Hello Mr. Darnell," Tion said, shaking his outstretched hand.

"Hello son, don't worry. This week will get better and to both you, don't worry about Bridget. They have been separated for over two years, I am sure someone told her you were back in town. She only comes around to stir the pot when she can. I am going to go back and take a quick look at my friend and then I will see you both tomorrow for the services okay?"

"Okay and thank you for the talk. See you soon." Tarilyn told him, waving slightly as she wrapped her arm around Tion's shoulder.

Anthony had made sure they were outside the door and out of earshot of anyone inside before he let go of Bridget's arm. She frowned, "Did I just hear you call that boy, 'son'?" Anthony sighed. He really didn't want to have this conversation with her, but it seemed his luck wasn't going his way.

"As a matter of fact, you did."

"Wow. You have a son."

"Why do you even care? That's part of the reason that we aren't together now, remember?

"Why would you say something like that?" she asked. Anthony hated that she was pretending to be so clueless. For years, he begged her to give him children. She told him it was something that she wanted when they were dating and first married, but what she really wanted was the status that came with his name. She cared more about his money. They only lived together as a married couple for four years and have been separated for two. The way she acted those years still bothered him. He wasn't expecting to see her today. "So which one of your friends told you about Tarilyn being back home?"

"I don't know what you are talking about."

"Mm-hmm. Well I am going back in and you aren't, so come on. We will talk later in the week," he told her as he walked her to her car. The snow was falling lightly, and he didn't have a jacket on. Bridget got into her car without saying anything else. Closing her door, she started her car, as Anthony stepped back. Rolling her window down she addressed him. "Anthony, we do need to talk, so don't keep me waiting," she said in a seductive voice, and full smile. He wanted to roll his eyes but refrained.

"I won't. It's time you got some papers from me, signed on my end of course," he said sternly. Her expression changed, and she rolled her window up quickly before pulling off. He watched as he got himself together to walk back in, he was greeted by Darnell.

"Hey, I'm sure you weren't happy to see her up here?"

"Not in the least bit. I am sure one of her friends opened they mouth."

"Oh, you know they did, I told Tari that same thing."

"Did you?" Anthony chuckled.

"Bridget is classic. We both know that. Tari doesn't, so I didn't want her more upset. Did y'all ever make that divorce final?"

"Not yet."

"Well you know what you have to do. Congrats on getting that son you always wanted. I am sure that had to make you very happy," Darnell changed the subject. Bridget was not a topic they needed to be discussing.

"You know, honestly it does but I am also terrified. Tion is almost a man, what can I teach him now? How can I benefit him? Tari clearly hasn't needed me to help her take care of him."

"More than you think you can't. If he is opening the door for you, you better walk through it. Most young men wouldn't even give this opportunity a chance. You are getting more than that."

"Yeah, you are right. Thank you."

"You're welcome. I'll see you tomorrow," Darnell told Anthony as they shook hands. Darnell pulled his coat closed and headed to his car. He was hoping he could heed his own words, and that his beautiful daughter would give him the chance Tion was giving Anthony. Darnell was still a little speechless, he made a promise he was now breaking. Yet he had a feeling this promise was meant to be broken at this time, so he was going to take it for what it was worth. Darnell pulled the picture out of wallet and ran his finger over Tara's face. He still missed her so much. She was everything to him, even at their young age. He never ever dated another woman on a serious level, he always compared them to his soulmate. Looking at Tarilyn all he saw was her, he would be a fool to let her leave without making her a part of his life. Wiping his eyes, he quickly got himself together. Starting his Cadillac, he slowly made his way back to his bar for the night rush as he shifted his thoughts. He hoped they could all get through tomorrow.

Almost the Last Goodbye

It had been a few minutes since Anthony went outside. Tarilyn was trying not to let the situation cross her mind. Hugging her son, they made their way back to the rest of the family. It was almost time for the viewing, and Tarilyn was mentally tired. Suddenly, she heard her name being called. Turning, she and Tion both saw Anthony lightly jogging to catch up to them. Tion gave her a look and kept walking. Tarilyn was hoping her facial expression wasn't showing what she was feeling. She really didn't feel like talking to him right now. When he caught up to her, she stepped back to separate herself.

"Anthony. I really don't want to do this now please," she told him softly. She was hoping the family wasn't watching them, as more members started coming in, and nodding to her as they walked past.

"Do what? I would never disrespect you like that. You should know that. Bridget and I are history and that is all I will say on that now. I will let you get back to the family. I can come over later," he told her, grazing her cheek with his lips, as he gave her a small hug. She knew that hug was what she needed. Sighing, she released him and walked to where Tanisha was standing, waiting on her.

Tion walked over and began talking to Anthony. She could hear them talking. She wanted to listen but knew that she shouldn't, so she used the family as a distraction.

Over the next three hours they were greeted by family and friends of their mother. Some Tarilyn remembered, most she didn't. Tanisha sat with her in a corner of the room of people laughing and talking. "Hey are you okay?" Tanisha asked.

"I am just tired, I'm sorry. I hope it's not showing."

"It is. Don't worry about it though, it's expected. What I need is a drink, I have a small bottle in my purse, come on, let's go do a shot," Tanisha suggested. Tarilyn softly chuckled at her sister but got up and followed her. Drinking wasn't her thing, but it seemed to be the only thing that changed her mood during this visit. Tanisha opened the ladies' room door and locked it behind them as she placed her purse on the sink and dug into it. She pulled out a pint of Effen. Tarilyn was astonished, she was thinking Tanisha was talking about the mini bottles. Twisting the top off, Tanisha handed the bottle to her.

"Here hold this, I have a shot glass in here too." Tarilyn held the bottle as requested. Her sister pulled out the shot glass and rinsed it. Taking the bottle from Tarilyn,

Tanisha poured the liquor into the glass. Raising it up she spoke, "This is for you Mama and Daddy. We love y'all." She downed the drink and poured more liquor, handing it to Tarilyn. Tari took the glass, closed her eyes and downed the liquid. It burned but tasted like it was coating her feelings. Her sister poured another shot and downed it. Looking back at Tari, she motioned to the bottle. "No, one is enough for me. Thanks," Tarilyn said. "I got some gum you want a stick?" she asked, as they rinsed their mouths and washed their hands. They were about to walk out the bathroom, when someone knocked. Opening the door, they were face to face with Stacy. "Oh, sorry I hope I didn't interrupt anything."

"No, you good. We were just coming out anyways," Tanisha told her.

"Oh okay, Michael was looking for you two anyways. He just walked up front," Stacy said.

"Okay thanks, we will go look for him." Tarilyn told her as the sisters' grabbed hands, smiling walking back to the room. The liquor was taking effect on her. Tarilyn spotted her brother and a few other men talking near the casket. She didn't want to walk up to the casket, so she paused, calling out to her brother instead. He walked over

114

to her and said, "Hey I just wanted to make sure you were okay. Anthony texted me and told me to check up on you. He told me you met Bridget."

"So you knew about Bridget?"

"Uh yeah, I went to the wedding."

"Wow, and you didn't think to tell me."

"I didn't think it was needed. You made it clear you were not talking to him, so I didn't think that you would care about what he was doing in his future. We weren't that close, but I mean… I was invited, so I went," Michael told her, taking her by the arm. Tarilyn almost snatched away but knew he was right. She had no right to be mad. He wasn't keeping anything from her. "I'm sorry. I am overreacting. It is just too much going on. I think I am going to grab Tion and head back to the hotel."

"He left with the other kids… told me to tell you he was going to stay at the house."

"Okay, well I will see you at the house tomorrow. Can you tell everyone else I am gone?" she asked, as she grabbed her things, and they headed towards the door. Michael nodded as he placed his arm around her. Wiping her eyes, she took a deep breath, briefly thinking she should have taken another shot with Tanisha. Placing her coat on, they increased their steps. It was definitely winter in Detroit; the front lobby held the cold air. Closing her coat, she stepped closer to her brother and he opened the lobby door for her. "You sure you going to be okay alone tonight?" he asked as they stood outside. "Yeah I will be okay. It may be good for me to be alone. I have food and a hot bath is in order." She told him as she looked around. "Shit," She mumbled.

"What's wrong? Where is your car?"

"That's what's wrong. I just remembered Anthony brought us up here, I don't have my car."

"Oh no problem I can take you."

"You sure?" she asked him, as they were about to make their way back into the funeral home.

"Mike, I can take her. You don't have to go out your way, a voice said behind them. They turned to see Anthony walking towards them.

"Oh, thanks man," he said to Anthony. He then turned to his sister, "You okay with that?" She hesitated but then nodded.

"I just finished my meeting and remembered I brought you up here," Anthony said directing his comment to Tarilyn. Michael squeezed her hand and then spoke, "Okay Tari, I will see you tomorrow. Thanks again Ant."

"No problem," Anthony replied. Placing his arm out, he motioned towards the door. Tari followed silently. Anthony opened the car door and she got in. She wasn't sure if she wanted him to take her back to the hotel, but it was only a short drive, so she would tolerate it. Once he got in, he kicked the heat up a few notches, turned on the radio, and pulled out of the parking lot. For the first few minutes the only sound in the car was jazz music. Anthony cleared his throat, breaking the silence. "Are you going to be silent the whole ride?" he asked.

"I don't have anything to say, I told you earlier that I didn't have anything to say about the situation. It still applies."

"Look, I know you are mad, and you do have a right to be. I should have told you about Bridget when we first started talking a few days ago, but I just didn't think it was relevant."

"Didn't think it was relevant? You're married Anthony."

"Separated… and we have been for over two years."

Married, separated, what's the difference? You are still legally bound, that's the point I am making."

"I know but I…"

"But what?" she interrupted, "You came at me like I was who you wanted. Like we were what you wanted."

"I do. If you sat there and told me that you were going to give us another chance, I promise you those papers would be filed on Monday." He grabbed her by the face softly. "You are all I have ever wanted. You left me, remember? I still love you Tari. I never stopped loving you." A horn blared loudly from behind them, making them both jump a little. Turning, he focused on the road as she replayed what he said in her mind. He just told her he loved her, but what that being in love or just love? The tears started to form in her eyes and she quickly looked out the passenger window. Reaching into her purse, she was about to pull out her Kleenex when she noticed they were pulling into the hotel parking lot. She was not surprised when he didn't take her to the front door, and instead he parked in a slot.

"You don't mind, do you? I was hoping we could continue talking for a little bit," he asked as he turned off the engine.

"Well you already parked, didn't you?" she said trying to sound indifferent. Leaning over, she attempted to take her seatbelt off and was greeted with Anthony's lips. He pushed his tongue in her mouth forcefully, yet gently as he tried to deepen the kiss. Her mind wanted to stop him, but her heart and body felt otherwise as she allowed the intrusion to her mouth. The kiss intensified and she felt emotions she hadn't felt in so long. She wanted to reach out to touch him but withheld, as she forced herself to push away. Anthony's eyes glistened. She licked her lips and then turned away, as she finished taking her seatbelt off. Opening the door, she reached for her purse and got out the car. The cold air hit her immediately, Tari's mind was full, and she just wanted to get up in her room. She didn't even look to see if Anthony was behind her as she made her way through the lobby. She got to the elevator and pushed the button when she felt his presence behind her. When the elevator opened, he held it open while she walked in. They didn't exchange words on the short ride up. Tari pulled the hotel card out of her purse and Anthony held his hand out. Looking at him weirdly, she didn't say anything. "The card," he said, motioning to her hand. Her first thought was to tell him "no" but she knew he was just being a gentleman. She handed it to him. After the doors opened, he followed behind her as they made their way to her room. Suddenly, she felt nervous. *"Was this really only going to be continuing a conversation?"* she thought. Standing in front of the door she waited until he opened it, as he held it open for her to enter first. She headed directly into the sitting room, where they discarded their coats. "Do you want a bottled water?" she asked him.

"Sure I will take one."

"Okay, give me a minute as well, I want to change," she told him. Walking into the small kitchen area, she grabbed a water out of the fridge. Handing it to him, she went to her room and closed the door. Sitting on the bed, she felt overwhelmed as she replayed the kiss and his words. He loved her? She didn't know what was going to happen, but she knew she wasn't prepared for any of it. It wasn't like she hadn't been with men since they split, but she never gave her heart on purpose. The next thing that ran through her mind was her promise. She promised to have this talk with him that concerned their son, but there was more. She changed into more comfortable clothes and got her mind ready for whatever conversation they were about to have. Walking back into the den, she watched Anthony for a second. He was deep into whatever movie he was watching. She slid onto the end of the couch and he turned his attention to her.

"There you are. I was just about to come knock on the door, I thought I had lost you in there."

"Lost me?"

"Yeah, I thought maybe you had fallen asleep on me."

"That wouldn't happen. So... you said you wanted to finish our conversation. I am listening," she said sternly. Tari thought if she came at him assertively, nothing would happen but the talk.

"You are getting straight to the point, aren't you?"

"Well, I am just going by what you said, right?"

"Yeah you are right. So, I have been sitting here thinking. Before we go into that conversation, I have a question for you."

"Question for me?"

"Yes, what do you want? What do you want between you and me?" Tari looked at Anthony and wished she had a mirror so that she could see her own facial expression. Why was he asking her this? This wasn't supposed to be about what she wanted. Did she want anything real with him? Her mind was so messed up, she really didn't know if she could provide him with an honest answer. She sat quietly. Anthony cleared his throat and she smirked.

"In a fantasy world, I want us as a family. In the real world, I don't know what we can have. I would love for us to just start over, but I really don't see how that would be possible with the distance and all." Tarilyn told him.

"If a man wants to be with you, nothing will be a diversion, including distance," Anthony told her as he moved closer to her and took her by the hand.

"When I told you that I loved you in the car, that is what I meant. I must have called your brother a million times, trying to reach you, and he would never give me your info. As much as I respected him for that, I was still hoping he would crack one day and just tell me, but he didn't."

"You did all that, really?" she asked, her eyes welling with tears. "Why? You didn't seem to fight to keep us together back then when I left. I thought you just didn't care."

"It wasn't that I didn't care, I didn't know how to. That was until I realized that you were really not coming back. I was a wreck. Then I just passed the time the wrong way… with women. I just put you out of my mind." Tari wiped her eyes but didn't respond to his comment. She took her hand out of his and stood up, walking towards the balcony door. She was getting nervous. Should she be just as honest as he was being? She felt him come up behind as he placed his arms around her. He lightly kissed her neck and she could feel little shocks going through her body. "Anthony…" she started. He shook his head against the back of her…

"Don't stop this. Let me show you how much I have missed you, how much I am still in love with you," he whispered, as he turned her around. He took her face into his hands as he bent down and kissed her softly and then harder, inching her sweater down her shoulder. He stopped kissing her and started licking her shoulder. Tarilyn's body began to feel hot. She wasn't sure if he wanted her to do anything to him, so she did what he asked… she just let him have his way. It wasn't until that very moment, that she realized how much she needed this. It had been such a long time since she had been touched by a man, and it was her choice, but this desire had been eating at her slowly. Anthony caught her off guard with the next thing he did. He swept her off her feet and carried her back into the bedroom. Laying her on the bed, he pulled her sweater over her head and pulled her pants off her all the while staring straight into her face.

Don't Spoil this Chance

Anthony looked down at Tarilyn's body and he smiled. She was so beautiful to him. Even though she was a lot thicker the last time they made love, he still liked what he saw before him. He pulled his shirt off and then leaned over her as he took her breast in his mouth, twirling her areola with his tongue. Her body arched and she moaned, it sounded like music to his soul as he increased the pressure on her breasts, biting and sucking on her. Anthony switched to her other breast and Tari grabbed him by his bald head and pulled him up to her. She kissed him hard and then he was the one moaning, he loved the way she kissed. Breaking the kiss after a few minutes, she gave him a sultry look with her bruised kissed lips. "Take them off," she told him motioning to his pants. He stood up and did as he requested. "Shit", he mumbled, remembering he had no protection with him.

"What's wrong?" she asked.

"I don't have any protection with me."

"Oh. Well go check your sons' bag, I make him carry it with him at all times, I am sure he should have something with him."

"Really, you make him do that?"

"Uh yes, I am not trying to be no grandmother yet," she told him as she nodded toward the other room. When he left the room, she quickly grabbed her ambience spray and filled the room with its scent. She wanted to make sure the room had the right feeling. Anthony walked back into the room waving the condom."

"See? You found it."

"Yep it was in his bag, just like you said it would be."

"Good, now hurry," she said, as she watched him sheath himself. Anthony reached down and placed his hands in between her legs and spread her wider. As he rubbed his finger up and down her clit again, she moaned. "You smell so good," Anthony placed his thumb on her clit and felt it harden, while his other finger gathered her wetness and helped him ease into her sweetness with two other fingers.

"Oh my goodness, stop teasing me."

"You ready for me?"

"Y… Yes," she replied as sexy as she could, feeling the anticipation. When he entered her, she gasped as they stared into each other's eyes. Then she felt her eyes roll as he sunk deeper into her wetness. Tari arched her back as they continued making love. Anthony stopped and had her change positions as he increased the speed of his thrusts. She felt like her head was spinning and her body about to explode.

Anthony watched her body respond to him and it made him increase his motions. If someone had bet him a few weeks ago this would have been happening he would have lost, but all the emotions that he had missed having with her were coming through him now. He meant everything he told her. He did still love her and had never stopped. He wanted a future with her and hoped that she would let it happen. When he was about to cum, he yelled out "I love you" as he burst inside of her. They collapsed onto the bed, and he held onto her tight as they snuggled. Tari closed her eyes as she listened to him lightly snore. That hadn't changed over the years. She kept replaying what happened in her head. It was different than it was 17 years ago, but why? Then the last conversation she had with her mother came popped into her head. She heard what her mother said about Tarilyn and Anthony, and how much she wanted Tarilyn to think about reaching out to him before she left. She wondered if things didn't occur as they did, would she have kept her promise? She couldn't honestly say that she would, she was fine with the way her life was. At least that was what she had been telling herself all these years. She didn't pine away for Anthony after their son was born, even as he grew up looking more and more like him. Tari needed some air. Her thoughts were getting to be too much. Softly, she took his arm from around her waist and got up, throwing his shirt on. She looked back and made sure he was still asleep. Walking over to the balcony door she cracked it. It was way too cold to go out, but the air was serving its purpose. How could he love her? The thought ran through her mind again, but she shook it completely. The most important thing was would happen once she leaves after the funeral services. She needed… no wanted to get back home.

Anthony moved in his sleep and was surprised that all he felt was the sheet, rolling to his back he let his eyes get adjusted to the dark as he looked around the room. Feeling the slight breeze, his gaze fell on the balcony door where Tarilyn was standing. He couldn't believe it. He'd actually made love to her again. After all these years, the one woman he wanted to spend his whole life with was back in it, and he wasn't going to lose her. He already knew what he had to do, and just hoped it would go smoothly. Getting up, he put his pants on and walked up behind her. Taking her by the waist, he pulled her close, "Are you okay? I could see you over here deep in thought" he said, nuzzling against her neck. Tari didn't respond immediately. She wasn't sure if she should tell him or keep the thoughts to herself. Without giving it more thought, she walked out of his embrace and headed back over to the bed. Patting it, she motioned for him to come and join her.

"Anthony, I promised mama that I would meet up with you and tell you about Tion, but it all happened so differently. I am happy that you and Tion will have a relationship, but us? What can we have? Honestly?"

"Why do you feel we can't have something? The distance?"

"It's more than the distance, you are married."

"Oh I see, but even though I said it's not a major concern?"

"You really don't understand do you, you really think she is going to be okay with us getting back together?" she asked, throwing her head down. Her irritation was starting to show in her voice, and Anthony immediately grabbed her chin, making her look back at him. "When I told you earlier that I loved you, I meant that wholeheartedly, and I can say it in front of her and anyone else I need to prove it to. Don't give up on us, please," Tarilyn was getting confused by all this. It was just becoming too much.

"Okay, you know what we are done talking about this for the rest of this morning. Mama's funeral is in less than four hours and I just want to lie down" she said as she swung her legs over him, pulling his shirt off, and laying still. Anthony sat still for a few minutes before he decided he would go home. Just like her he needed to prepare for the next few hours ahead... He already had the papers drawn up, he would have them served while he was attending the service.

Fully dressed, Anthony leaned over and kissed Tarilyn on the cheek. She didn't move or respond. "I'll see you in a few hours," he whispered. Letting himself out, he headed to his car. He reached his house in no time and didn't even remember the short drive. Kicking his boots off, he went into his office and picked up the paperwork.

He and Bridget met the last year that he was a pro basketball player. She walked into the room and literally every man's mouth flew open. It wasn't that she was *Top Model* gorgeous, it was more how she captivated them with her appearance. She walked right over to him and started talking. They dated for six months straight, saw each other daily, and then he proposed. They had a nice sized wedding and great honeymoon, but after that everything changed. She always traveled, never spent any time at his games, and when he got injured, she was really a ghost. That's when he asked her about having children and she came up with every excuse in the book not to have any. That was his breaking point. He always talked about it with her and she was so animated with her responses but was lying the whole time. He was devastated. When he had to leave the industry, he immediately started his own company. For the last five years, he had grown in one of Detroit's top law firms and for him that was his baby… until now. Signing the last page, Anthony placed the papers in the envelope for delivery, heading upstairs he went into his bathroom, hitting the knob for the shower. He understood what Tarilyn was saying and the last thing that he wanted to do was add more to her plate on top of the grief she was already going through he thought. "Well let's see what the rest of this day holds," he sighed, as he climbed into bed to try and rest.

Tarilyn's alarm was going off, hitting the button she got up and was feeling groggy, when did she even fall asleep? She felt the kiss from Anthony and heard him leave. Her tears took over and that's the last thing she remembered. The tears weren't all for him, it was everything. She wasn't expecting to come home for Christmas and have all this happen. Getting dressed, she said a quick prayer and headed to the church.

Tarilyn was determined to get through this day as best she could. She texted Tion as she got on the elevator. She rubbed her forehead, she felt her phone vibrate in her hand, looking down as the door opened, it read: *"I'm here."* She glanced around the lobby and she saw Anthony standing by the entrance with food and coffee in his hands. He was dressed in a suit and looking handsome. She couldn't help but smile. She was still confused on what she was going to do regarding them, but she wasn't going to think about it now. He handed her the coffee cup as they walked out in silence to his car.

"Thank you for the breakfast. That was very thoughtful of you. I hope you have eaten or are going to eat as well," she said before handing him a breakfast sandwich. Kissing the back of her hand, he took it from her. Tarilyn continued to sip her coffee and eat before they made it to the church. They listened to the radio in silence as he drove. Pulling up to the church, they parked where they were directed. She wasn't surprised to see it was packed, their mother was heavy into the community and served on a lot of committees. "Are you okay? Ready for this?" he asked her softly.

"As much as I am going to be, I just honestly want this day over."

"Yes I can understand that, I'll help you get through this as much as you allow me to."

"Okay," she told him as they prepared to get out the car. Once she opened her door, Tion was by her side in minutes. She could see the pain all over his face, he was dreading this as much as she was.

Anthony hung back and let them walk in with the rest of the family. He watched as they slowly walked up to the casket once again. Tion broke down first and then Tari followed. His first reaction was to go to them, but her brother beat him to it, so Anthony decided to go and sit down. He saw Darnell and sat by him. It bothered him that

133

he couldn't be the one to console them. He and Darnell made small talk throughout the hour-long service. They were about to stand for the last prayer when Anthony felt his phone vibrating in his pocket. Looking at the screen he rolled his eyes, Bridget had gotten the papers. Her text in all caps read, *"SO THIS IS WHAT WE ARE DOING NOW? THAT BITCH GOT YOU WANTING TO END US NOW? YOU SURE ABOUT THIS? 'CAUSE YOU WON'T BE SOON!"* Without responding he put the phone back in his pocket. Instantly he wished he had waited until Tarilyn left, but he had to show her he was serious. He would deal with anything that occurred. Darnell noticed his facial expression and tapped his arm. "You okay, man?"

"I think I am. I had Bridget served with the papers this morning, and she isn't happy. I guess I wasn't expecting this much flack from her," he whispered.

"Aw man, yeah I don't know how to help you handle that one, but I warned you it would happen. She's okay as long as she still has some control over you. That divorce will take that away from her, and you know she doesn't want that."

"Yeah I know. I just won't think about all that now. Hopefully it won't come back to bite me later,"

Anthony said as they filed out of the church. He shook hands with Darnell and told him he would see him in a little while. He waited for Tarilyn by the car as they greeted family and friends outside. He felt his phone continue to vibrate but he didn't even bother to look at it. After about ten minutes Tari and Tion both headed to his car. He let them both in and silence was housed in the car on the way to the cemetery. He did hold her hand the drive and was surprised and happy that she allowed it. When they got to the cemetery he opted to stay in the car, Tion bent his head over the seat, "Mom, is it okay if I stay in the car?" he asked her. Touching his cheek, she nodded yes. Getting out the car, she walked toward the rest of the family.

Taking the Wrong Step Forward

Tion sat back in the seat and wiped his face. He never thought he would have to say good bye to his biggest hero. His grandmother did so much for him, even with the distance. It just dawned on him that she wouldn't see him walk across the stage in a few months. It hurt his heart more. He tried to hold the tears in but was unsuccessful. Anthony reached over into the back seat as much as he could as he tried to console him. "Tion I promise I will be there for you, I want to make up for our lost time." He told him as Tion nodded.

"She won't be there for me, I am going to miss her, and now she won't see me graduate. Will... will you be at my graduation?" he asked through tears.

"Of course, I will. I will be down there every month, if it's okay with your mom. I know this is hard on you, and I want to try and ease this pain as much as you both will let me."

"Momma, she will let you, she wants to fix this too."

"Well that's good to know, but we will take it slowly and step by step." Anthony told him as he released

136

him. Tion wiped his face and was getting himself together when Tarilyn got back into the car. The repass was back at the church in their large hall room.

"How are you holding up over there?" he asked a little into the ride back,

"I don't know. I am a little bit worn out, but I know we still have a few hours to go. I still can't believe that she is gone. I was just expecting to come and spend the holidays with her and the family. Now we have to spend it without her," she replied. She replayed the last few days over in her head, and it just seemed unreal. Reaching the church hall, they all got out and walked into the hall where some people were already seated, and others were helping with the food setup. Tion went to where the rest of his cousins were and Anthony took her coat as she went to help the family, who immediately turned her away. She was greeted by Tanisha, "Come on little sister, follow me." She told her taking her by the hand. Into the back they went, and immediately Nisha pulled out her famous remedy bottle and her two shot glasses, pouring them to the rim. Clinking the glasses, they gulped it down, and followed by another one, she was glad at that moment she had something on her stomach, the liquor burned going down, but she had to admit it made her feel better if only for that moment.

"That should hold us over for a little while. If you need another one, just come get me."

"Okay, thanks. We needed that. I think we all did better than expected today, what do you think?"

"Yeah, we did okay, at least one us had a little extra of a support system,' Tanisha said nudging Tari who blushed.

"I wasn't expecting that, or with Darnell but I will handle all that later. Let's get back out there and get some food. We will definitely need to talk later," Tarilyn replied. Tanisha was putting her bottle back in her purse when they heard yelling coming from the front. Hearing her name being called by a female voice. The sisters walked out of the bathroom and saw Darnell and Anthony holding Bridget.

"You can't have him! Who do you think you are waltzing back in town and thinking you can change my life? His life? You can't have him, I said!" she continued to yell. Anthony was saying something to her but no one else could hear.

"I don't care about no timing!" she yelled. "Let me go, I've said what I needed to say anyways." Turning around she glared back at Tari, as the room remained quiet. "I don't back off easily, just know that. Oh, and by the way, sorry for your loss," she spewed sarcastically, heading back out towards the exit. Tarilyn covered her mouth and thought the liquor was going to come back up. This was not something she was going to deal with, and she instantly made up her mind about Anthony. Looking at her brother she motioned for him to address Anthony. She walked quickly into the back. Her brother walked quickly to where Anthony was standing. He knew who Bridget was, and knew that was normal for her. She always had to be the center of attention, not even caring who she was hurting or what she was disrupting. He should have addressed her when she was there. Michael pulled Anthony off to the side with a look of disappointment. "Man, we don't know what the heck that was all about, but we already dealing with enough. I think you should just go. No need to make it worse, she's even more upset now." Michael told him. Anthony didn't say anything. He knew Michael was right and turned to leave, but Darnell stopped him. "I'll walk out with you. Michael I will be back in a few minutes, go ahead and say grace," Darnell told Anthony as they started

139

walking. Reaching the top door, they saw Bridget speed off out of the parking lot.

"I don't know what you thought you were going to accomplish by handling this situation like this. You know how she is. I can't tell you what to do because you can't erase what just happened. I will tell you this, if Tari is like her mother was, you probably just messed up any chance that you had to win her back."

"But..."

"Let me finish. Did you really think it would have been that hard to sit down and talk to your wife first?" Anthony's face twisted a bit, but Darnell continued.

"Yes, I said wife. No matter how long you two have been separated, fact is she is still your wife. I know you don't want to be with her, but you could have gone to her and brought it up in an adult conversation. Let her know enough time has passed, instead of having her think the whole reason was because of Tarilyn. You just swallowed a barrel of sour grapes, son. I've always seen you as an intelligent man, but this right here was the dumbest thing you have ever done," he told him.

Anthony let all he said sink into his head, and he knew he was right. When he saw her walk into that hall, he, knew it was going to get ugly. He didn't' handle this right. Now he had to fix it in not one but two women's eyes.

"Can you tell her I'm sorry?" Anthony asked, walking to his car. Sitting behind the wheel, he didn't know if he should go home and sulk or try and fix whatever issues his wife had. He pounded on the wheel a few times. He didn't want to lose what he was recreating with Tari, but did he just mess up everything he was starting anew? If what Darnell said was true, then he did, but he wasn't going to just let it go. He couldn't. Pulling out of the parking lot, he headed to the place he knew his spoiled ass wife was going. He tried to prepare himself for whatever would happen when he got there. He hit his turn signal and headed down Jefferson. The house they started to build together sat halfway completed. Her car was in the driveway. He parked, got out, and tried to put his key into the lock on the front door. He was surprised it didn't fit. "What the hell?" he thought. Trying not to be pissed, he knocked on the door. After a few minutes, she snatched the door open and walked away. He closed the door and followed her.

"So, you changed the locks?" he asked.

'And? Why do you care if I did?"

"This is still my house," he retorted.

"Oh yeah, I guess it is…" she said frowning up at him. "Why are you here anyway? You made it clear I am not what you wanted."

"Bridget, I came here to apologize and talk, I handled this wrong and I just wanted to tell you why."

"Why? You made that abundantly clear, you want to be with her."

"Come on now, you are treating this like I am cheating on you. We haven't been sleeping together for the last two years, you aren't any more in love with me than I am you. So just sign the papers so we can go on with our lives like we have been."

"Wow, so now you want to be the adult in this situation. Tsk, tsk, tsk. What do I get out all of this?"

'Ahh I see that's what this is really about. Tell me what, exactly do you want?"

"This house, my car, and alimony for at a least a year, I mean I can think of a few others," she counted off on her fingers. He shook his head wondering how he even fell in love with, let alone married this woman.

"So that is all it takes, huh? While we are being honest with each other, why don't you finally answer me this: Why did you lie to me? Why did you tell me you would give me kids when you knew you wouldn't?"

"That's not entirely true."

"Explain that because you dodged me on this subject for over a year." Anthony said. He instantly saw her demeanor change. She went over to the table and sat down, placing her glass in front of her. She looked defeated. It was a look that he had never seen on her face before. After a few more minutes, she finally began talking.

"It… It wasn't like that. I just didn't think I would be a good mother, I never had that motherly feeling like my other friends did. I didn't grow up with a mother or a father for that matter. My grandmother raised me, and she didn't show me a parent's love. I didn't want to disappoint you nor whatever child we brought into this world. I owe you an apology for not telling you the truth. I just didn't want to ruin what we had then. I just thought maybe you would get the picture sooner or later." Anthony stood there with his mouth wide open. He would have never thought of the reasons she gave him, it made him see her in a different light. He just wished she would have just talked to him that would have made it better.

"So what's next?"

"I'll have my lawyer look over the papers after you have them revised, and then we can go from there."

"Oh okay, I will get that done, let me get out of here. Thanks for the calm talk, again I apologize for how this went down."

"Yeah, I guess I am over it now," she told him as she took a sip from her glass. Standing up she walked behind him as he headed to the door. When he reached the door, he turned around toward her and was caught off guard by her next action. Bridget grabbed him by his shirt collar and pulled him towards her face, opening her mouth to bring him towards her aggressive kiss. Anthony could not get himself out of her embrace. Without better judgement, he kissed her back. As the kiss deepened, it sank into his head what he was doing, and he yanked away from Bridget. Wiping the edges he backed away.

"What was that for?" he asked sheepishly. He hoped he could play it down and get out of there before the whole scene turned into something he didn't want. Bridget kind of laughed before she opened her mouth to respond.

"To let you know that I am still the one who can get and keep your attention, at least I thought I was. What does she have that I don't?" she snapped.

"It's not like that. Why do you think all this is because of Tari?

"Because I never had to try and get your attention before she came back in town. Now look at this shit. She comes, and now you are all in, and I won't talk about what I heard. She gives you the one thing I didn't give you. How fucking convenient. You know what? I am done talking, just go! I wish I could take my kiss back!" she shouted, at him as she wiped at her mouth, taking the back of her hand she started pushing him out the door. As Bridget slammed the door on his back, he could hear her yelling through the door, but couldn't make out what she was saying. He stood there in the cold, wondering what the heck just happened. He knew that getting this divorce wasn't going to be easy after all. Getting into his car he started it and grabbed his phone out of his seat console. He had chosen not to take it in, just in case he got a call she would trip on. He had three missed calls from his son, and a text message. Dialing the number, it rang once before going to voicemail. Replying with a text he dropped the phone and pulled off, heading in the direction of his home. Thinking over the last few hours, Anthony felt defeated. He didn't want either Tarilyn or Bridget to be upset with him, but he knew where his heart was. He had to fix things with Tarilyn before she left, and he didn't even know when that was. Pulling into his driveway, he sat there. He didn't even recall the drive home; his thoughts were everywhere. Reaching over to grab his phone, he jumped as it started to ring. Hitting the button he saw that it was Tion, "Hey son, is everything okay?"

"Not really, mom says we are leaving tomorrow night, if she can finish what she needs to do of grandma's stuff. I just thought that you should know," Tion told him. Anthony sat there with his mouth agape, kicking himself.

"Okay, where are you now? Still at the church?"

"Yeah but we are cleaning now, I am going back with my cousins. Mom said she wanted to be alone, so was heading back to the hotel when we all got done. Dad can you fix this? Tomorrow is Christmas Eve, and I want to be here for Christmas. I was hoping that I would get to spend it with you, but she said she didn't want to talk about it. She doesn't even know that I called you. Please."

"Yeah, I will try my best to, I was hoping the same thing Tion. I will talk to your mom tonight if I can. I will call you later, okay?"

"Okay. Thank you," Tion told him as they ended the call. Looking at the dashboard, Anthony saw that it was only a little after four o'clock. He decided he would let her have some space and then go by the hotel later in the evening.

Stay, Don't Go

Tanisha saw Tarilyn sitting at the table by herself, she hadn't said much to anyone since the scene with Anthony's wife. Grabbing her purse she headed over to where she was sitting. "Let's talk. Well listen, I just want to give my few cents on all this. Now first, we can't undo what happened earlier but shit, it could have been worse. What you need to decide is what you are going to do, give it a chance or let it go. We all know Anthony was your heart. Do you still have feelings for him?" Tanisha asked, as she poured them a shot. Tarilyn sipped it before she answered her sister.

"I do, but no matter the feelings, the fact is he isn't single. I won't stand in the way of him having a relationship with Tion. As far as with me? If I did, this mess today kind of decided it for me."

"Tari, come on now. Give him a chance to at least tell you his side of the story."

"Why are you so team Anthony?"

"Now wait a minute I didn't say all that, but I know that you haven't dated in the past few years. So at least give him a chance to tell you his side of the story."

"Yeah whatever, I don't know about all that just yet. Maybe I will just head back to Atlanta tomorrow."

"Tomorrow?" Tion said interrupting their conversation.

'Tion, what are you doing listening to our conversation?" Tanisha said.

"Auntie, I was just coming over to let you both know we were almost done and ready to go. Then I heard what my mom said."

"Tion, we will talk about this later. Are you staying with your cousins?" Tarilyn asked.

"Yes if that's okay."

"Yes I am going back to the hotel to have some quiet time. I may come back out, but I will let you know," she told him, before he kissed her and walked away.

"Sis don't leave tomorrow. That wouldn't be good for us or for you. We don't want you to leave, tomorrow is Christmas eve. We still need to be together as a family. That's what Mama would want," Tanisha told her. Tarilyn just shook her head. She knew they weren't going to leave tomorrow but she needed that to be what got back to

149

Anthony. She could still see their mother laying in that casket this morning. Even with the drinks, talking, drama, and family, all she still felt was pain. She felt the pain of knowing she wouldn't be able to call her mother and hear her voice, and not seeing her at all anymore.

"Hello Tari, you listening to me?" Tanisha asked, snapping her fingers in front of Tarilyn's face.

"I'm sorry," Tarilyn said.

"What are you thinking about?"

"Just seeing mom in that casket, knowing that it's the last time I will see her."

"Yeah. I just wasn't expecting all this, I mean not right now."

"Who you telling? I don't know how I am going to get through this," Tarilyn sighed.

"Oh you will, we will, together. Pinky promise." Tanisha told her holding her pinky finger up. Tari grabbed it and they laughed. It was something they always did growing up. She missed those moments.

"Go get some rest. I am about to go have another drink with my friend. I will catch up with you later or see you at the house tomorrow, okay?"

"Okay. I will think about it and yes I will see you tomorrow if nothing else, love you."

"Love you back." Tanisha told her. They hugged, and Tari immediately tried to keep the tears from falling. Tarilyn went to grab her coat and Michael came over and helped her. "Are you okay?" he asked.

"I will be. Thank you for handling that earlier."

"No need to thank me, it will blow over though. Bridget has always been messy, but I am sure you already know Ant is a good guy. I want to see you both happy together or apart," he said, hugging her.

"Thank you, I will see you tomorrow," she told him. Some of the family members were going back over to Michael's house, but she really didn't feel like being bothered with everyone. She wanted some time alone. It was something she had not really had since their mother passed. Reaching into her pocket she realized that she had her keys, but not her car. She was just about to ask Michael to drop her off, when Darnell smiled and waved at her.

"Do you mind dropping me off at the hotel? Anthony was driving us around today, and I just remembered that," Tarilyn said.

"Of course, of course. Come on," Darnell told her. Waving to everyone they all headed out the church. Darnell held the door open for her as she got into his car. He turned the music down and pulled out of the parking lot.

"I still would like to have some one on one time with you and Tion before you go," he said.

"Well, from all that happened today I was thinking maybe it was best if we just head on back home. I don't think I could handle anything else."

"I understand, but please don't let that determine the rest of your trip. I know this wasn't how you were expecting anything to be. But the bad can turn into so much good, starting with me getting my daughter back, and your son gaining a dad and a grandad. Have you had a chance to tell him yet?"

"No, I was going to just let it happen when we all got together. I am afraid I will be throwing too much on him," Tarilyn sighed.

"Pretty much like yourself huh?"

"Yeah, I guess you are right about that. But all that doesn't break you, just makes you stronger right?"

"That's a good way to look at it, you sound just like Tara and Darlene. Both sisters had so much resilience in them, it just makes my heart swell thinking about them both."

"Tell me about her please. What would she do if she was in my shoes?" Tarilyn asked.

"Well one thing is for sure, if Tara was here, she probably would have snatched Bridget's behind up, but Darlene would have done what you did. Not make the situation worse. They were both so different, and held their own."

"Why did you let me go so easily? Didn't you want me in your life?"

"Tarilyn. Don't ever think I didn't think about you daily and regret the decision I made. I wasn't prepared, back in those days, things were so different."

"This is all just confusing. I never expected all this coming home. I knew one day I would have to face the truth with Tion and Anthony. But finding out about you and Tara. It's like I don't know what to feel. I feel a lot of things and still just digesting in along with losing mama."

"I know babygirl. I hope that you will give me the chance to work with you in sorting it all out." Now Anthony. I have some concerns for you and him, especially when it comes to Bridget, she's always been a troublemaker and in all honesty, I think if she loved him, she would've just took it step by step. It's always the easy route to just throw in the towel, you just have to follow your heart. If what you feel for him is what I saw all over both your faces this week, I would say don't give in so quickly; yet hold your ground and don't be forced to make any decisions either. You deserve to be happy; but a love from a man doesn't mean happiness. That comes from here first." Darnell told her pointing to her head and then her heart.

Tarilyn shook her head and in understanding and then took in a deep breath and wiped away the tears that were forming.

"That was the same thing Michael said. Growing up I never thought I was pretty. All the boys and men for that matter went after Tanisha, and she soaked up the attention. I always felt because I was thick, I wasn't what they wanted, then when Anthony came along, he showed me how to be a friend, that's what we were from the beginning, what a real friend was. That's what I treasured the most, and it just grew from there."

"Funny, that's how me and Tara were. She was my tutor, and we were just friends but would sit up and talk for hours. Until one day I took a chance and kissed her, then we were inseparable from them on. When she got pregnant with you, our families were so mad, yet still supported us. I was so ready to be a husband to her, even as young as we were. She was my everything, my light, my darkness, my strength, my weakness, my sunshine. My everything. If he makes you feel all that, then keep him, even if it's just as a friend." Darnell told her.

Pulling up to the hotel as the conversation ended. Tarilyn this time didn't hide her tears. It was like she felt her real mother come over her when he spoke those words. Darnell leaned over and wiped away her tears. In return she took him by the hand and placed in her heart, leaning over and kissed his cheek. "Thank you," she said.

"For what, sweetheart?" Darnell asked.

"For giving me the definition of love. I wish I could bottle up how you loved her. It shows all over your face, and in your voice. That's a rarity."

"She was a rarity. Just like you are. You are beautiful inside and out. I hope you allow me to be a part of you and Tion's life," Darnell said.

"I most definitely will."

"Good, good. I am thinking about planning something for tomorrow. I know its last minute and won't compare to what you all are used to, but I want us all to be together."

"Okay. Just call me with the details and thank you for the ride and conversation."

"No, thank you for the opportunity to be in your life. Meeting you could have went a whole lot of different ways, but I prayed and prayed, and God answered me this one time since losing your mother, Tara and I am truly blessed." Darnell told her.

Tari got out the car and headed into the hotel room. As she was heading to the elevator, she decided they would stay as planned. Texting Tanisha, she waited for the elevator to open. Smiling at the quick response from her sister, Tarilyn stepped inside the elevator, hearing her name being called as the door closed.

Promises, Promises

Anthony had to think of a plan, something that he could do that would make Tarilyn believe in him again. It was all becoming a little more than he had thought about. Then he remembered the card Darlene had given him. She told him not to open it until she was in heaven. Rushing into the house, he threw his coat off and went searching for the card. It took him about fifteen minutes, but he finally found it. Ripping the envelope open, something that was in the card fell out and hit his feet. Looking down he was shocked to see what it was… a necklace. In fact, it was the one that held the engagement ring he had given Tarilyn when they were in college. Picking it up, he ran the length of it through his hands. He opened the card and opened the small note that was in it. He began reading what Darlene wrote: *Anthony, I am hoping by now you are getting to know your wonderful son, Tion. I kept a lot of things from Tarilyn, and I know that's taking a toll on her. Now, I just want you to fight for her. Whatever happens while she is*

here, please fight for her, she needs you more than she will
admit. She has always been the strong one in the family,
but never had anyone to be strong for her. When you were
dating, you were that for her. She left this necklace on her
dresser when she moved, and I just took it. I am sure she
would love it back. Take care of my baby girl and
grandson. Thank you!

Darlene

Anthony wiped the tears from his eyes. Darlene had found
him when he was at a low point. The conversations they
had were a saving grace for him some days. He wished he
knew all of the things Tarilyn was dealing with, but that
was the smallest part. He saw the strength Darlene spoke
of, but he also knew Tari wasn't as strong as she made it
seem. He heard it all in her voice and saw it in her face
over the last couple of days. Opening his hand, he put the
ring on the small part of his finger. He thought back to the
day he gave her the ring and the necklace. The sparkle and
love that he saw in her eyes, made him happier than he'd
ever been. He wanted to see that again, he had to. Making
up his mind, he put both the card and necklace on the table
and walked into the kitchen. He poured himself a drink and
he sipped on it lightly. Going into his office, he pulled up

the divorce decree on his laptop, making the adjustments he had talked to Bridget about. He then sent it over to Bridget. He wasn't even sure if she was going to sign it now. He wasn't sure why her mood changed as quickly as it did. Recalling the conversation, it still just made him think about the time they were married. He wondered if she ever really wanted or even loved him. She was always caring more about what he brought home. He wanted to just wash his hands of her and this so-called marriage they still were holding on to. Today was turning out to be one crazy day, he thought to himself as he finished off his drink. Standing up he began to pace his office. The words of Darlene's note rang in his mind. Anthony knew what he was going to do, and just hoped it would go his way. Exiting his office, he took the stairs two at a time as he unbuttoned his dress shirt and threw it in his basket. Turning on the shower, he checked his phone. Tion let him know he had made it back to the house safely. Anthony was happy at least one person wasn't upset with him. He tried to clear his mind and heart as he let the water cleanse him. He had to do this… if not for him, for the promise he made to Darlene.

***

"Ms. Johnston, you have a delivery," the delivery person told her as he handed Tarilyn a bouquet of flowers. Taking the flowers from him, she instantly inhaled their scent, already knowing who they were from. Thanking him, she headed back towards the elevator. Smelling the flowers again, she smiled against her feelings. She was still upset, but the flowers were helping her mood. Opening the door to her hotel room, she was instantly caught off guard. She was greeted with candles everywhere and something all over the floor. They weren't petals, that she could see. Bending over she saw they were seashells., She picked one up, they were small but beautiful.

"Do you like them?" she heard from the sitting area. Startled, she turned and was face to face with Anthony.

"You know I do, but… how did you get it here?"

"I told the guy I left my key with you. So with some convincing, he gave me one," Anthony smiled.

"Wow Anthony, why though? Why are you here?"

"First to apologize about Bridget's behavior earlier, and to hopefully help you relax and talk. I know you are still mad at me, but please let me stay," Anthony pleaded.

He watched her place the flowers down and take her coat off. Tarilyn was confused, her mind wanted him to leave of course, and her heart was telling her to let him stay. When she didn't say anything, Anthony moved out of her sight and was back in a few seconds with a glass of wine and a plate of chocolate covered strawberries.

"What's all this?" she asked.

"Come on follow me, I told you I wanted to help you relax, and this is part of it," he told her as he led the way into the sitting area. Tarilyn's mouth flew open when she saw what he had done. There were more candles, there was a robe, and oils laid out on the table, she noticed that he somehow got a massage table setup in the room by moving the furniture in the room. All this was for her? The tears clouded her eyes, and she covered her face.

"Tari why are you crying?" he asked her as he wiped her tears from her face with his hand.

"Be... Because you did all this for me..." she responded through her sobs.

"I told you, I love you and this is a way for me to show you. Despite what happened earlier, you have had a rough last four days, so I wanted you to unwind some. Now go ahead and bathe. The water is still hot and ready. Let me know when you are ready to come out please."

"Okay, and just in case I forgot to tell you, even though I am still upset with you, thank you for all this, and the effort you are making," she said, heading into the bathroom as instructed. Anthony couldn't do anything but smile. He almost danced around the room, but like she said she was still upset. So he had to do more to gain more status with her. He finished preparing the items he would need for her massage. He lit the candles around the area and refilled her glass as he heard her calling his name. Stepping into the bathroom he saw Tari wrapping herself in the towel. He had to keep himself from walking over to her and touching her.

"Ready?" she asked.

"I hope so," she laughed lightly. Taking her back into the room he stood to the side so that she could see the setup in full.

Tarilyn's eyes grew large in surprise. She didn't know what exactly to say, but her mind was racing with questions. He did all this for her? Why was he doing all this? She placed her eyes on Anthony who was motioning her to come over to the massage table. She walked over and lied down before she unhooked the towel and let it fall. Anthony raised the table and stood over her. Warming his hands with the scented oil, the smell filled the room. When he touched her skin she almost jumped, she was startled that it was heated. He started at her shoulders and rubbed her gently as he covered both her sides. She closed her eyes and tried not to moan out loud as the massage was feeling so good. It had been a long time since she had a massage, let alone the treatment he was giving her. He worked on her body for another 30 minutes, before he asked her to turn on her back. He laid a sheet on top of her and started at her feet and worked himself upward.

Anthony was trying to control his body as he worked on hers. He was upset with himself because this wasn't supposed to be about him. This was all for her, so if anything happened, it would have to come from her initiating it, not him. He closed his eyes and willed his body under control, especially when she turned on her back. His mind flooded with thoughts of the times they used to have, and the one they had the other night. He knew she was the one for him, and he didn't have to remind himself of how he loved her. He would do just what Darlene asked of him, fight for her! Once he finished the massage, he retrieved her robe and turned on some music.

She joined him in the sitting room and hugged him from behind.

"Thank you, I didn't realize how much I needed that, I feel so relaxed now," she said.

"Well I knew you needed it, so you are very welcome. I have a little surprise for you, and I hope it won't change the mood."

"What is it?" she asked anxiously. He pulled her around him and reached into his pocket. "Close your eyes, please." Closing her eyes, she stood anxiously. Anthony placed the necklace on her and latched the hook. He saw her touch it as she opened her eyes looking down,

"Where… where did you get this?" she asked him in complete bewilderment. She turned to face him holding onto the ring on the necklace.

"Darlene. She told me to fight for you and said that she thought you might like it back."

"She did what? She gave this to you, but how?"

"You left it, and she took it," Anthony replied.

"Yeah, I remember now. I did leave it, but I thought I lost it. I didn't see it when I went back home after Tion was born. I just put it out of my mind."

"Do you love me?" Anthony asked.

"Yes, I love you. Am I still in love with you? As crazy as it may seem I believe I never fell out of love with you. I just pushed the feelings out of my thoughts, but it never left my heart," Tanisha answered.

"You just don't know how happy that just made me feel..." he started but then Tarilyn put her hand up to stop him.

"Anthony, we can't do anything about these feelings. You are married, and I would be hurting myself if I even put myself in that position. So please don't attempt to do that to me or even yourself at this point."

"I know but I talked to her after I left, and she agreed to sign the papers. So, we are halfway there. I won't push anything you don't want, but I am just saying, don't give up on us please. There is a reason why we are standing here, I can't break my promise to your mother. It is my promise to keep," Anthony told her as he pulled her into his arms, leaning down to kiss her. Without hesitation Tarilyn kissed him back. Anthony thanked Darlene in his mind, as he held Tarilyn tight in his arms deepening the kiss.

Breaking the kiss, he heard Tari's stomach growl. "I take it you didn't eat earlier?"

"Not really I wasn't in an eating mood, but I guess my stomach is telling on me," Tarilyn laughed, slightly embarrassed.

"Well I will fix that, sit down and relax and give me a few minutes," Anthony told her. Sitting down, Tarilyn looked down at the necklace and thought back to when he gave her the ring. It was after one of his games and he was the star of the game. Even with all the attention that night, he came straight up to her and picked her up off her feet swinging her around. When he placed her on her feet, he got down on one of his knees and the school mascot ran over and handed him a box. He proposed to her in front of everyone. They were sophomores and decided afterwards that it would represent both engagement and a promise to marry. She was so happy and in love with him then, he was her everything. Smiling, she continued to think about the love they had back then. Anthony cleared his throat breaking into her thoughts, blushing she looked up and he was carrying a tray with a full meal and glasses of wine.

They talked as they ate, and when they were finished, he brought over the container that held the chocolate covered strawberries. "May I?" he asked. She nodded in response as he fed her one of the strawberries.

"These are so delicious. Thank you for all this."

"You deserve it and more. Now you know what else you deserve?" Anthony asked, smiling.

"Oh my, what else could you have for me?"

"Just my arms, you deserve to be held until you fall asleep," he told her softly. He shifted his body so they could lie comfortably on the couch. He held her and they listened to each other breathe.

You Deserve Love Too

Tarilyn didn't remember falling asleep but she opened her eyes and was surprised that she was in the bed, not on the couch. It was almost five o' clock in the morning. She turned on her side and was disappointed to learn she was alone in the bed. Did he leave? Throwing the covers off of herself she got up and walked towards the kitchen area. Smiling she heard the light snoring before she saw him lying on the couch. Getting some water, she walked back into the bedroom and sat on the edge of the bed. Holding the necklace in her hand, her heart skipped a beat. It was the first time she wished she could go back in time and change how things played out between them. In four days her whole life seemed to change, and she wasn't sure how it was going to pan out. She was terrified, not just for herself though but for Tion. He was all she had the last 17 years. She knew that their bond couldn't be broken but now with Anthony in the equation, she wondered how that would change things. Shrugging her shoulders, she pushed the questions out of her head for the moment. Grasping the ring and sliding it onto her finger she looked at it, and her heart began to swell with emotions. Without thinking, she said "I love you," barely above a whisper.

"And I love you." She jumped when she heard his voice behind her. How long had he been standing there? Turning slightly, she saw Anthony standing on the other side of the bed. "You scared me," she told him.

"I didn't mean to."

"How long have you been standing there?" she asked.

"I just walked in actually, at the right time it seems. You want to talk about this some more? I know last night you said some things that we both already knew, but Tari, I can only do what you let me is the bottom line."

"I... I know, and that is what scares me the most. Anthony, no man has ever done what you did for me last night. I can't explain how much that moved me. I keep replaying it in my head, and what got me is that you weren't expecting anything in return. I mean it's always a catch, normally," Tarilyn said.

"My goal is to show you how a woman should be treated. From our high school years and while in college, I always wanted to make you feel special, and I didn't know how fully. I made the mistake of letting you go when we were younger, and not only did I lose the last 17 years of my son's life, I lost almost a lifetime with you. I have never let you go from my heart, so like I told you before I just want the opportunity to show you. Darlene had faith in us, and she is watching us hoping we don't break our promises, the ones we promised to keep." He held out his hand to her and Tarilyn let him pull her up. Her arms went around his neck and she couldn't hold her tears in. Her mother did this for them, and she owed it to her to give him a chance.

"Let's do this slowly and see where it goes," Tarilyn smiled through tears.

"I don't want to sound like a broken record, but I will if that is what proves all this to you. I will go as slow as you want us to. Thank you, Tari."

"Come on let's lie back down. For once I don't have to get up early. This will be the first Christmas eve that I won't be talking to my mother. I hope I can get through all this," Tarilyn said as she laid her head on his chest. *Christmas Eve… guess she had to go out and get Anthony a gift,"* she laughed to herself.

"You will. You got me and Tion. Now get some sleep, it's going to be a long day." He told her. Tari instantly closed her eyes and he watched her as she slept, shifting his body so that they could both be more comfortable.

Anthony finally dozed off but before he could get into a deep sleep, the sound of a ringing cell phone startled him, waking them both up. He reached for his phone, but it wasn't his. Tarilyn picked her phone up, spoke and then sat up.

"Hi… yeah I was but it's okay today? Okay, yes, we will be there, we will see you later. Okay talk to you later." Ending the call Tari placed her phone back on the night stand.

"That was Darnell, he is having an impromptu Christmas Eve gathering tonight and wanted me and Tion to come."

"Oh yeah? Speaking of Darnell I have been meaning to ask you about him." Anthony said in a tone she hadn't heard before.

"Him? Oh you mean Darnell? I guess I just assumed you knew…" she started but was interrupted by the beeping of Anthony's phone. He started to ignore it, when Tari motioned for him to go ahead and look at his phone. The text was from Darnell, inviting him to the Christmas Eve gathering. "Guess I am going to, just got my invite as well," he told her as he laid the phone face down. "So back to what you were saying, what did you assume I knew?"

"Darnell is my father. He was with my real mother Tara, who is actually my mother, Darlene's sister. She died while having me."

"Wow, that's a lot to digest," Anthony sighed.

"More than you can imagine, this week has been full of twists and turns."

"Yeah, I see. I hate I added to it."

"Let's not talk more about that please. I am starving though, you want something? I am going to order from room service," Tarilyn said.

"Sure I will have whatever you are getting. So what are you doing about Darnell?"

"Pretty much what I am doing with you, taking it day by day. He told me a lot of things I didn't know yesterday evening. If nothing it won't hurt me to listen and give him a chance. My mothers are gone, the only father I knew is gone. So it's like a new leaf. Same as you are getting with Tion," Tarilyn said.

"Well I guess you are right. Good Luck with it."

"Thanks, I am going to get dressed before the food comes," she told him, grabbing clothes from her suitcase and leaving him in the room. Anthony sat, thinking. Darnell was her father... so he had guessed right. He was amazed at how Tarilyn was really handling all this. If he was in her shoes, would he? It just made him even more sure that he had to be a shoulder for her. She needed it whether she showed it or not. Anthony went back into the room where his shoes and items were. He picked up all the things he used from yesterday. When he was done, he went back into the room and Tari was on the bed.

"So I have everything cleaned up from yesterday. I am going to go home and get some things done, and I will see you later tonight," Anthony said.

"Oh okay. Are you okay?" Tarilyn asked.

"Yeah I am. I just wanted to go and get Tion a Christmas gift."

"Oh okay. I will see you later then," she told him. Anthony kissed her on the cheek, and she waved to him. She didn't bother to walk him out. Her mind was wandering. She wanted to get him a gift, but she didn't

173

know what to even get. She picked up her phone and called Tanisha.

"Hey Nisha, you feel like going to the mall with me?" Tarilyn asked.

"Yeah that's cool. I talked to Darnell this morning, are you going to the party tonight?

"Yes I am. I will pick up Tion and change at the house. Did you want to ride with me?"

"Doesn't matter, he said I could bring a date, so we will see. I will be ready in about 30 minutes," Tanisha told her.

"Okay see you then," Tari said before hanging up. She texted Tion and told him she was heading to the mall and would come and pick him up later. Tarilyn walked past the mirror to get her coat and stopped. Looking at herself, she could see how worn she was. Her strength was wavering, and she didn't know if she was going to be able to stay as strong as she normally did. Her mother was her best friend. They talked almost daily. Here is was day six and she didn't know what to do or how to feel. Her heart was in pieces, and this time she didn't think she would be able to fit the pieces back together. Trying to shift her thoughts, her thoughts went to Anthony. What was so special about her, that he wanted her so much? She lifted her sweater and looked at her stomach. It wasn't flat, but it was better. Every time she was asked out, she just knew it was an ulterior motive for it. She never let her guard down, she never saw herself as what a man would want. The one thing she noticed was that Anthony still did the elements of courting her. He always took her on dates and showed her what it meant to be on a date, like he did last night. Hearing him tell her that she deserved it made her heart full. The men she did meet in Atlanta would only do dinner and a movie. She became tired of that and just said she was better off alone. Applying some lip gloss, she made up her mind that she would take it slow with him, but he had to keep his word and go through with his divorce before she would do anything.

"Okay, I am going to do this," Tarilyn said aloud to her reflection.

"Girl this Detroit weather is a trip. When you got here it was freezing and now here it is almost 55 degrees," Tanisha told her jumping in the car.

"Yeah this is something that I don't miss at all."

"I bet, I am going to come down there next winter," Tanisha said.

"Come on, you know you always welcome. So let me tell you about last night…" Tarilyn started as she proceeded to tell her sister everything that happened with Anthony last night.

"Wow I am impressed. I haven't had a man date me in a while, it's all about that Netflix and chill shit. I am too old for that mess. What happened to dating? What happened to courting? That is what we grew up on, and these men seem to have forgotten all that," Tanisha said.

"Yeah, that's funny I was just thinking that same thing when I was getting dressed. I remember how daddy used to bring momma flowers home every week, how he danced with her in the living room just because, how they cuddled on the couch and had conversations, when they thought we were sleeping."

"That was the essence of dating. At least it used to be. I go to clubs and dudes wait for women to approach them to dance. My girlfriend told me that nowadays men want us to ask them out on a date, instead of them asking us. I just say wow."

"So what is your love life like? Are you seeing that guy I saw you with on a regular basis?" Tarilyn asked.

"Who? Brian? Girl no, he is the king of Netflix and chill. Yet, he gets mad at me when I say I am going out or want more. It is what it is, for the moment. Right now, I just need to be held until I can get through this a little more. Then maybe I will try something different, like online dating. One of my friends has met someone and they are going strong."

"Online dating? You not afraid of that? I mean, I have a couple friends who tried it, but they all had horror stories. Just be careful."

"It's still a thought, but no I am not scared. You know I am a huge risk taker. So I will go with the flow, if I go that route" Tanisha told her, as they parked and got out of the car.

More than You Bargained For

Walking through a few stores, Tari found what she was looking for, for both Darnell and Anthony. She took a couple of the pictures she found of Tara and Darnell and had one of them engraved and made into a bracelet, and the other into a huge framed picture. They were delivering it later. Tarilyn and Tanisha were tired, and about to walk out the mall when Tanisha nudged her. Walking in their direction was Bridget and a man. They were holding hands and deep into each other. Tanisha quickly pulled her phone out and snapped a picture. Just as she did that Bridget looked up, with wide eyes as she spotted them. Stopping in her tracks, her whole facial expression changed. The man she was with turned to Tarilyn and Tanisha who kept walking. Tanisha glared, daring her to say anything.

"Ladies," Bridget said as she got herself together. She let go of the man's hand, and he gave her a look of surprise. "So I guess you will be using this in your favor," Bridget said to Tarilyn.

"In my favor? Listen you don't even know me, and I don't know you. I didn't get at you yesterday because I am dealing with my mother's death but, trust me, you already used your one time to disrespect me," Tarilyn warned.

"What…" she started to say but was stopped by Tari's look.

"You look like you are enjoying your life, so why don't you let others enjoy theirs as well? Have a good holiday." Tarilyn grabbed her sisters' hand and they walked past Bridget and her male friend without another word. As they were passing them, Tanisha bust out laughing. They could see the steam coming out of Bridget ears. High fiving each other, they made it the car and headed back to the house.

"I am proud of you Tari, you handled that beautifully."

"You know I am not a confrontational person, but she was out of line yesterday, I needed her to know I wasn't weak."

"Oh, trust you did. So, let's change the subject how are you going to handle these men in your life now, Darnell and Anthony?" Tanisha asked.

"Honestly, I don't know about Anthony just yet. I feel like it's all new to me, I am still so unsure. As far as

Darnell, I want to know as much about Tara and him as possible, so I will welcome the relationship. Hopefully it will help with the grief."

"Good, you know I got you on both levels," Tanisha told her. They got to the house and relaxed before it was time to head to Darnell's club.

Anthony put the bags down. He had gone to get a few outfits for Tion, he hoped he would like them. Then he opened the case and looked at the gift for Tari, he instantly got nervous. Anthony was hoping things would progress the way they talked about. A friendship was something that he could accept and make more, but he was going to take a huge chance and accept if things didn't go the way he hoped. Changing clothes, he headed to the club. Walking in there were a few people there and he greeted them. Scanning the club he was looking for Darnell. He took a seat at a booth and the waitress came over and asked him what he wanted to drink. Ordering he decided to text Tari.

Hey, are you headed this way soon?

Yes, I am headed there in a few, waiting for Tion to get dressed.

Okay see you soon.

Anthony saw Darnell and waved. Walking over they shook hands, "So you have a daughter and a grandson, old man."

"Yeah, I do, a blessing in disguise. So how did you handle your situation?" Darnell asked.

"I went and talked to her, and then I pampered Tari. I am hoping that both work out in my favor."

"Oh I am sure you do. But if Tari is anything like Tara. Don't look for it to be easy breezy. You are going to have to fight for her love and she is worth it."

"Yes, she definitely is. I got this," Anthony told him, sliding it across the table.

"Whew," Darnell whistled. "Son, you sure about this?"

"More than anything!" Anthony replied as he placed it back in his pocket. Darnell watched Anthony as he responded. His immediate thought was he was doing too much. He wished he could get him to see things through his eyes. It wasn't that he didn't deserve to be happy, but he was moving too fast and that would cause him to be on the short end of the stick. Darnell learned a long time ago not to try and tell these young men too much. They didn't listen, they thought they had all the answers. When did they stop learning and wanting to learn from the older men in their lives? They used to soak up all the knowledge from their elders. Now what they got was the guys combating what they said, instead of welcoming the knowledge.

"Alright son, I wish you the best on this. Let me go back here and check on the food and remaining preps before the rest of the people get here. There are no tabs tonight, so enjoy.

"Thank you," Anthony told him, sipping his drink. He thought about what Darnell said. He wondered if he was moving too fast. The sound of the phone vibrating on the table broke into his thoughts. Turning it over he was surprised and disappointed that it was Bridget.

"Hey, what's up?" he asked.

"Hey, I will make this short, I will go ahead and sign these papers, and send them to my lawyer, and we can go from there."

Oh, okay uh thank you," Anthony said. Bridget ended the call without saying anything else. Looking at his phone, he was completely in shock. He looked into his glass as if it was spiked.

"What the hell just happened?" he said aloud.

"What was what?" Tion said from the side of him. Anthony didn't see them all come in, at least twenty strong. The whole family walked in together. He stood up and hugged Tion, then his son sat down. Tarilyn and Tanisha walked over to the bar and Tanisha ordered her usual. Tarilyn turned down a drink for the moment, she needed to eat first. She walked around the club admiring the decorations. She felt Anthony behind her before she could even turn around. "I know you just walked in but let's dance." He said to her smiling hard. Laughing, Tarilyn let him lead her to the dance floor. As they started to dance, they were quickly joined by other family members. They danced to about three songs straight before she was spent. Darnell had the food out and they headed over to make a plate. "You know, it feels so good to see you smile. I truly missed that genuine smile," Anthony said.

"Stop you are making me blush," Tarilyn said, smiling.

"Go ahead, it makes you radiate even more."

"Oh so you are laying it on thick huh?" Tarilyn joked.

"Naw, just telling the truth."

"Oh okay I hear you. By the way I saw your wife today."

"Really? Where was this?" Anthony asked.

"The mall. It was interesting, but I said what I needed and left it at that."

"So did what you had to say, have anything to do with her calling me and saying she was signing the divorce papers?" Anthony.

"I don't know, but I guess that works out for you now," Tarilyn shrugged.

"No it works out for us both," Anthony said. Tarilyn didn't say anything, but what he said was neither true or false. She did tell him he needed to be unmarried before they could pursue anything, but was she ready for what he wanted? She let the question resonate in her mind as she finished her dinner. The next few hours the family celebrated, danced, and had genuine fun. Tarilyn realized it was something they all needed, and she appreciated Darnell for doing this last minute. Looking at her watch, she noticed it was almost midnight. "Mom, come here," Tion said motioning to her to head towards the stage, where he, Darnell and Anthony were standing. Hesitating slightly, she walked up to them.

"What's going on?"

"Well I just wanted to express how grateful I am to have you in my life, even for the short amount of time, so I wanted to give you something." Darnell said first. He reached on the side of him and reached into a bag, inside he pulled out a box. "I want you both to open it together." He motioned to Tion, who took the box and began opening it. Inside the box was a huge plaque in the form of a heart that housed all of their family's names. It was made of gold and silver, and it was beautiful, Tarilyn was speechless. "Son don't know if your mom told you yet, but I am your grandfather, and this right here is for you only. He handed him an envelope. Tion opened it, and on the inside were a set of keys. He looked at his mom, Anthony and then back over to Darnell.

"It's a start up car, but it's something for you for the moment."

"Darnell, oh my that is so sweet of you," Tarilyn said.

"Yes, thank you so much." Tion said in shock, shaking his hand. Tanisha walked up to the stage with him.

"So let's keep the momentum going. Our family wanted to thank you for all this, but Tari wanted to do something extra special for you..." she started.

"Yes, Darnell this night means too much to us, traditionally we always spent this together with our parents, and always with our mother.

After our conversation I wanted to get you something you would be able to see daily and think of love. So, here you go," Tarilyn told him as her brothers walked the huge framed picture and uncovered it. Darnell gasped as he looked at collage of pictures of himself and Tara, laughing, hugging, and posing. Tears immediately filled his eyes. Tarilyn handed him the box and he opened it, taking the bracelet out and placing it on his wrist.

"I... I can't say how much I love these both. You are truly a treasure," Darnell said, leaning over and kissing her on the forehead. Accepting his kiss and hug, she was just about to walk off the stage when a song came on that made her stop. Slowly turning around, she was greeted by Anthony on one knee and Tion standing right by him, slightly on his knee as well. Holding a beautiful blue topaz and diamond ring in his hand. Tion was smiling so hard, it made her heart feel even more, she wanted to say something, but Anthony started talking before she could…

"I know this maybe too soon, but all I know is that my life is incomplete without you, and I know without a doubt that I just want to go half on forever with you. Will you be my best friend for life?"

Epilogue

A little over a year later

Tanisha walked into the room and gave her sister a hug, she was glowing. "So you ready?" she asked her. "Yeah, I am. You look beautiful, being pregnant looks good on you. I can't wait to meet my nephew," Tarilyn told Tanisha, and she rubbed her seven-month-old belly.

"Too bad it doesn't feel good on me, but look at my baby sister, you look absolutely stunning."

"Thank you, I am still in awe. This last year has been a whirlwind. I just wish our parents could be here to enjoy both of our moments."

"That I agree with, but we will make the best of it anyway," Tanisha told her as the coordinator walked in and told them it was time. Tanisha hugged her quickly and followed her out the room. Picking up her bouquet, she headed towards the door. Darnell was standing their waiting on her. "Baby girl, you look radiant." Tarilyn replied, "Thank you. You don't look bad yourself."

"Yeah I ain't too bad for a seventy-year-old man," he told her chuckling taking her by the arm, as they stood at their cue point. The garden was lavished with lilies and orchids, her favorite and their scents filled the whole outside. Everyone stood up and the music started, as the vocalist began singing. Darnell walked his daughter down the flower filled pathway. Anthony watched as Tarilyn made her way down the aisle towards him. Tion was his best man, and to him the moment could not have been better. When he proposed on that Christmas Eve, he was surprised and a little devasted when she turned him down in front of everyone. Yet he was forewarned, he just thought she would believe in him, and eventually she did. The last year was hard but the best he ever had. He'd gotten to know Tarilyn and Tion better, and it was truly all he could have asked for. Taking her hand from Darnell, Anthony stood in front of Tarilyn and had to keep himself from kissing her. The pastor looked over at him and then to Tarilyn.

"Are you ready to read your vows?" he asked. They nodded. Their vows were going to be a little different, they decided to intertwine them. He would say one line and she would follow

The day I met you was one that can't be replaced, even though we were kids, I knew then you were for me.

You gave me something I thought I always lacked…
unmeasurable love.

You are my best friend.

My other half,

My soulmate,

My life mate,

And together we made a promise to keep, that has given us
strength, love, and devotion.

Today I say I do.

Today I say I do.

"Now after that the only thing that is left to say is, I now
give you God's children, and pronounce you Husband and
Wife. You may kiss your bride.

THE END

You can reach out to Jada Pearl:

www.TheBeamCreativityLounge.com

@authorjadapearl on Twitter, FB and Instagram

Email:authorjadapearl@gmail.com

Check out Jada Pearl other titles

Made in the USA
Columbia, SC
21 October 2023